HEART'S HOLIDAY

HEART'S
HOLIDAY

•

JAN McDANIEL

AVALON BOOKS
THOMAS BOUREGY AND COMPANY, INC.
401 LAFAYETTE STREET
NEW YORK, NEW YORK 10003

PRINTED IN THE UNITED STATES OF AMERICA
ON ACID-FREE PAPER
BY HADDON CRAFTSMEN, SCRANTON, PENNSYLVANIA

HEART'S HOLIDAY

Chapter One

Sharon Hunicutt's gray-blue eyes widened with horror as the flash of black metal cut across her field of vision. With dull certainty that her efforts were hopeless, she had time to do no more than press the brake with her foot and await the inevitable scrape of metal against metal.

Her dark lashes fluttered shut, blocking out the horrible reality of the impending crash. It was something apart from her she heard, something she saw coming, a movie of sorts. Fleetingly, she wondered with what seemed to her amazing calmness, whether she was going to be killed. But it was a question without time for fear or regret or answers.

Numb, all she felt was a grating, rocking sensation that seemed to go on forever. But one small word echoed from the center of her soul—no!

1

Her heavy leather briefcase and camera case slammed off the passenger seat to the floorboard.

After the longest few seconds of her life, a sudden stillness fell over the world.

Dazed, she stared through the cracked windshield at a black wall of metal. Slowly, her senses began to return enough to force her to look down at her body. With great relief, she saw no blood. She wondered whether there was pain or whether she was too numb to feel it yet.

Grateful for her habit of routinely snapping her seat belt, she cast an eye at her belongings scattered on the floorboard and killed her engine. Then she surveyed the damaged windshield. She was alive, she was unhurt.

With what seemed a huge effort, she unbuckled her seat belt. Abruptly, her car door swung open.

"Are you all right?" A deep voice demanded.

Startled, she looked up into a pair of the warmest brown eyes she'd ever seen and a face carved with the ruggedly handsome features of a movie star. The image was somewhat fuzzy, and she assumed she was hallucinating.

Her mouth fell open, and she groped for words.

Before she could speak, the stranger took hold of her arm and was urgently pulling her out of the car.

The sudden motion set her head reeling, and

as she got to her feet, she raised a trembling hand to her forehead. She wobbled forward and thought she might have fallen over if the tall man hadn't caught hold of her.

"Did you hit your head?" he asked, scanning her delicate face for signs of an abrasion, his broad hands still propping her up.

"I don't think so," she said, trying to focus better on his face. "I was wearing my seat belt."

She felt embarrassed at the unaccustomed intimacy of being held up by this stranger. "I was fine before you pulled me out of the car."

Ben Russell studied the women who felt slender and small beneath his grasp. Her silver-plated eyes fringed in black against creamy skin cast a striking image, one he knew he would not soon forget. An oversized fisherman's sweater tented her long legging-clad legs. Although her clothes were casual, he could tell they were expensive. She smelled faintly of designer perfume, jasmine and a hint of musk.

He glanced at the briefcase on the floorboard. A businesswoman passing through on her way to Atlanta, he guessed. He knew the type all too well, people who think everything important in life revolves around a conference table and a travel schedule. He pushed the thought aside. He wasn't going to let his feelings about Yvonne cloud his judgment right now. The right thing to do was help this woman and get her on her way.

"I didn't think you'd want to stay inside the burning wreckage."

"It's not burning," she said pointedly.

He shrugged, releasing her. "Go back and sit inside if you like," he offered obligingly. "Some friends of mine have already passed by and said they'd call the police. They should be here momentarily."

She glanced back at her battered car meshed into the side of the black pickup truck. She had no desire to return to the wreckage.

"That's your truck?" she asked.

"What's left of it," he said, planting his hands in his pockets. As if struck by a second thought, he pulled his right hand out of his coat pocket and offered it. "Ben Russell," he volunteered.

Sharon hesitated.

"Surely you don't blame me for this," he suggested when she failed to accept his friendly gesture.

"No, that red car came barreling through the stoplight and set my car into a spin when I tried to brake."

"That fool," Ben muttered, reaching out and grasping her unyielding hand, shaking it firmly. "Whoever he was, he's long gone. It was no one from around here, I assure you."

Sharon tried to ignore the electricity that sparked up her arm at his touch. She reminded herself she was extremely vulnerable right now, not thinking clearly. This irrational attraction she felt was solely in her imagination. After all, he had, in a manner of speaking, rescued her.

"I hope I'll be able to drive my car."

"I doubt that, Honey," he said, appraising the wreckage.

"My name isn't Honey," she snapped. She detested being talked down to.

Ben's eyes danced. He could tell she was upset, and he'd been trying to make her feel better, not offend her. "If you'd tell me what your name is, perhaps I could call you by it."

Sharon tapped one flat-clad foot on the concrete. It was two days before Thanksgiving. She'd hoped to attend to her business here and get home tomorrow. She and Chris had important plans for the holiday.

And now she was stranded in a distant north Georgia town where she knew no one except this impossible man who seemed determined to take charge of her and looked better than anyone had the right to. The way he unnerved her was annoying.

But when she looked up into those intriguing eyes and smooth compelling face, she realized he was partially right. She had failed to identify herself.

"Sharon Hunicutt," she said with a light laugh.

He flashed a dazzling smile that made her heart jump.

"Pleased to meet you, Sharon. If you can laugh about this, you can laugh about anything. I think we'd be better off if we got out of the street."

He began leading her toward the curb.

She followed, glancing down the unfamiliar streets. She stood beside him on the curb in front of a fast-food restaurant. A cold gust of wind made her shiver. She folded her arms protectively across her chest.

The late afternoon sun had about given out and the darkening sky was frothy with gray clouds. An earlier rain had slickened the roads, and the bright lights of the restaurant reflected brilliant colors on the ground. She remembered the way her car pirouetted out of control earlier, sending her on a grisly merry-go-round ride. She was lucky to be standing here, she realized, seized by a more violent shuddering.

Tears welled in her eyes, but she fended them off. She didn't want this stranger to see her crying.

Hands brushed her shoulders, and she turned to see Ben Russell slipping his parka over her.

"I have a coat in my trunk," she protested, guilty at the sight of him in shirt sleeves.

"We can get it later," he assured her. "Are you certain you're not injured?"

"I'm not certain of much of anything right now," she answered shakily. "And I haven't even asked about you."

"Me?" he asked with flaring eyes. "I'm tough as leather." He lowered his voice and added, "But it's not an experience I'd care to repeat."

His surprise at her question indicated to Sharon he'd been too worried about her safety to have given a thought to his own.

A passing car slowed, the driver calling out to Ben.

"Excuse me," he said. "I'll be right back."

She watched him walk away, admiring his determined, straight stride. It was Ben Russell's presence that was keeping her calm through this, she realized. He had every right to feel as irritated about the accident as she initially had. Instead, he'd been concerned only for her well-being. She'd have to remember to tell Chris how caring these small-town people were.

She stared down the row of neat brick storefronts, the sprawling magnolias and oaks lining the streets. There was an aura of peace and antiquity here. Under other circumstances, she might have liked it. Now, she felt as out of place as if she'd landed a spaceship on Mars.

How would she get home if her car wasn't operating? She looked in the direction Ben had gone, missing his somewhat soothing presence.

She gathered her wits. She'd always managed to survive on her own and would do so even in this miserable situation. After all, she wasn't helpless. She just needed to modify her plans.

Another cold gust of wind swept over her. How she longed for her centrally heated cozy apartment with her scented bath oil, terry-cloth robe and fluffy comforter on the bed. Why was everything going wrong all of a sudden?

A misty rain began to fall—it had been raining intermittently all day—and it added a glistening sheen to the glorious scarlet and golden hues of the trees.

She drew in a deep breath. Autumn didn't look like this in Pensacola. She'd been driving against this backdrop for hours now and paid it little attention.

Tiny raindrops beaded in her silky shoulder-length brunette hair and across her lacy eyelashes. She blinked them away, simultaneously staving off an involuntary and unexpected swell of tears. This was the absolute last thing she needed. She had expected to complete her business here tonight and be on her way home in the morning. She'd been right on schedule until this happened.

Her stomach cramped so furiously, she unconsciously moved one hand over it.

Cars began pulling over, people getting out and rushing over to Ben, offering assistance. Everyone seemed to know him, she realized.

In the midst of a conversation with an elderly couple, he turned and looked her way. Then he led the little delegation over to her.

He introduced the older couple as the Boyces, then informed her they were willing to phone anyone she needed to call.

"Yes, thank you," Sharon answered. "I have an appointment with Sara Eagleston. I'd really appreciate it if you could call and tell her I've been delayed."

Ben's eyes flared. "You're from the museum?"

Bewildered that he would know this, Sharon nodded. "You know Mrs. Eagleston?" she asked. Well, he did seem to know everyone else here.

"She's my great aunt. She's been bubbling for a week over your arrival."

Sharon turned to the neatly groomed couple that stood head-to-head a full six inches below her. "Could you please tell her I'm here, and that I'll call her myself after things here are settled?"

She hoped to talk to the artist tonight and still leave on schedule somehow tomorrow. But a glance at her car told her there was a dim chance of that unless she left on a bus.

The small round woman with tightly permed salt-and-pepper hair stepped forward. "Can we call your family for you?" she offered.

Sharon hesitated. "I don't know anyone here," she admitted. "I've just driven in from Pensacola."

"We don't mind calling long distance," the man with thin white hair skirting his perfectly round head volunteered in a soothing, grandfatherly voice.

Sharon considered. She certainly didn't want to alarm her aunt and uncle in New Mexico, who could do nothing for her and would go wild with worry. Her sister, Blake, in Tallahassee, would immediately leave her family and her Thanksgiving preparations to drive up here, a totally unnecessary gesture. She entertained the idea of calling Chris. His presence would be comforting, but she was reluctant to selfishly take him away from his work. Her boss, Millicent, would come in a flash if requested, but Sharon didn't want to trouble her either.

No, the situation was under control. To notify anyone would only cause undue worry. As usual, she would handle matters herself.

She chewed her lower lip, and it tasted of rain. "No, there's no one," she insisted.

She caught the incredulous look Ben flashed her, quickly diverting her eyes from his. Something in his expression made her uncomfortable. Was it sympathy? Did he think she was totally alone in the world?

Right now, she felt as though she were, and maybe she didn't want him to see confirmation of that in her face. It was ridiculous, of course. She had as full and happy a life as anyone.

She wondered what Ben Russell did for a living. In his workshirt, jeans, boots, and the baseball cap that shielded his eyes from the heavy drizzle, she guessed he might be a farmer. People in these small towns just automatically knew everyone, she reasoned. It was a strange concept to someone who had grown up in a city where one only occasionally ran into neighbors or schoolmates.

She felt his eyes still on her. "I don't want to inconvenience anyone when there's no cause for it," she said as though he and the Boyces had pressed her for an explanation. "But thank you."

As flashing blue lights appeared far down the street, the Boyces left on their errand. Sharon's slim hand clutching the edge of his parka tightened into a fist.

The remaining sunlight faded fast, and the darkness dropped an aura of unreality over the scene. Someone, she thought it was Ben, set a styrofoam cup of steaming coffee into her hand. Even though she didn't like coffee, she drank it because it was hot and revived her somewhat.

She would not, she determined, sink in to self-pity over this. She would arrange to somehow carry on her business and get home in time for the holiday. She and Chris were driving to his parents' home in Panama City for dinner, and she would meet them for the first time. It was the one bright spot in her life she could pull out and hold on to right now.

She was mortified when an ambulance arrived, the paramedics checking out both her and Ben.

"She was dizzy when she got out of the car," Ben informed the paramedic, who was cracking a steady stream of jokes that made her laugh so hard her head hurt.

Finally, after she reluctantly admitted the buzzing in her ears and the pain in her stomach, he informed her she should go to the hospital emergency room and be checked by the doctor.

"I'd rather not, if it's optional," she said.

Ben, overhearing, came forward. "I wish you would," he said. "I feel somewhat responsible for this, and I'd sleep better tonight knowing you're officially all right."

"You're not responsible," Sharon told him. Still, his concern touched something inside her.

And never having been in a wreck before, the pain in her head and stomach did mildly worry her. Her expression tightened as she looked at her car, still in the roadway.

"The wrecker will take your car wherever you want," he assured her. "I'd recommend Towers Garage. He's the best in town."

She took him at his word, trusting his judgment instinctively, and gave her instructions to the officers after it was demonstrated to her beyond a doubt that the car was not drivable.

Feeling ridiculous, she climbed into the back of the ambulance. Darn that Ben Russell, she knew he was right. She too wanted the official certification of knowing she was as physically fit as she had been when she left home early this morning.

"Take good care of her," Ben instructed the emergency medical technicians.

Sharon reddened as he waved and flashed her a wink. She was unaccustomed to such quick and easy familiarity. Worse, coming so casually from Ben, she halfway liked it.

Sharply, she realized she was taking her last look at the big, compelling, caring man, and a sense of loss filled her. He was the kind of man she would have enjoyed meeting if, as he had suggested, circumstances had been different.

Quickly, she swung her thoughts to Chris, the

man with whom she'd frequently discussed marriage lately and who she believed was on the verge of proposing to her. Guiltily, she willed herself to stop upsetting her life with these vagabond thoughts.

"Sure thing, Mayor," the EMT promised.

Sharon's surprised eyes honed in on him, flashing back to Ben before the door swung shut and erased him from her view.

"He's your mayor?" she asked.

The EMT nodded.

She digested this new information, then dismissed her own keen curiosity. It didn't matter, of course, because with the closing of that door, she'd seen the last of him.

Chapter Two

Several hours later, after a distracted, harried young doctor ran tests and informed her there was nothing wrong with her except her own stress over the accident, he gave her an envelope with a tranquilizer in it and released her.

Now that it was over, Sharon found her head clear and her stomach suffering from nothing more than a gnawing hunger, since she'd stopped on the road for an early lunch and missed dinner.

Her body ached with a weariness as if she'd engaged in strenuous exercise earlier. She stuffed the tiny envelope containing the pill into her pocketbook, unconvinced she needed the medication.

She wandered into the lobby, scanning the corridor for a pay phone where she could call a cab, if this tiny burg had one, to take her to the motel where she had made a reservation last week. From there, she would call Mrs. Eagleston and see if she could arrange a meeting in the morning.

If her car could be repaired quickly, she might still be able to leave tomorrow and arrive home late Wednesday without upsetting her and Chris's plans for the holiday.

Disbelief rippled through her as her searching eyes lit on a now familiar flannel-clad figure fidgeting in one of the plastic chairs. As he spotted her, his huge smile tugged at her heart—a heart she believed was clearly reserved for another. He rose.

"They brought you here too?" she asked.

"No," he answered. "I came to see if you needed a ride anywhere."

She looked down at his feet and saw her briefcase, suitcase, and camera bag stacked on the floor. What kind of town was this where the authorities turned a person's possessions over to the care of strangers? she wondered. That overstepped even a mayor's authority.

She made a note to ask Chris about this point of law when she saw him again.

For now, she was glad Ben had brought her things to her. And too tired to decline his offer of a ride.

"Surely you're not able to drive your truck so soon?"

"No. John Towers, the garage owner, gave me a lift home, and I have my car. The truck was a company vehicle."

"I hope you won't get in trouble with your boss for wrecking it."

Ben flashed a heart-stopping grin. "I doubt that. I am the boss."

"Oh." Tiredly, she added, "I would appreciate a ride to the motel, thank you."

He lifted her suitcase and eyed her keenly. "You hate this, don't you?"

She looked at him intently, unsure what specifically he was referring to.

"Being in a wreck?" she asked.

"Accepting help from people."

"I'm used to being on my own, if that's what you mean."

He shrugged. "It doesn't hurt, when you really need it."

She reached for the briefcase and camera bag before he could get them. "But I hate having you go through so much trouble on my account."

Ben shrugged. "Not that much happens around here. Besides, we don't want you to go away thinking ill of the town."

The corners of Sharon's finely sculpted mouth lifted slightly. She shot him an amused glance.

"I wouldn't blame the entire population for one daredevil driver," she assured him. "If that's what you mean. The town's reputation is safe."

Ben led her toward sliding doors that opened magically when she stepped on the mat. Cold air blasted into the brightly lit corridor, and she quickly stepped outside.

"Over here," he instructed, gesturing with his head. She followed his lead, suddenly remembering she was wearing his jacket.

"I don't suppose Mr. Towers mentioned my car to you?" she asked.

"No. I'm sorry. You can call him first thing in the morning though. I did tell him you were anxious to get it on the road. He's good, but he can't work miracles."

Her eyes dropped as they reached his Grand Am.

"Look," Ben assured her, "don't worry about it until you talk to him. I'm no expert on automobiles."

He opened the passenger door for her. She stepped inside and watched as he stowed her things in the trunk and walked around to the driver's side.

"I hope you won't think poorly of me, Mr. Russell. Everyone here has been very kind to me, but I do have a pressing schedule."

"I understand," he answered in a tone that

didn't include approval. "Who wants to be stranded in a two-horse town two days before a holiday, or anytime for that matter?"

Her hands danced in her lap. "Well it's not that I have anything against this town, or any other," she tried to explain. "I just have a really important engagement for Thanksgiving."

Ben started the engine, and the heater blew in a welcome stream of warm air.

He cast her a sideways glance before pulling out. "You're one of those people who are always rushing, aren't you?"

Color rose to her cheeks at his accusing tone. "I lead a very busy life. I'm assistant director of the children's museum, and it's a demanding job."

She didn't like defending herself to him, and wondered why she was doing it with such fervor.

Ben shrugged. "I've just noticed that a lot of people who rush around a lot aren't really going anywhere, like a hurricane stalled out at sea."

"Well, I'm not one of them," she stated, wondering why his calm observation riled her so. It was just that—he didn't know anything about her. "Maybe you have me mixed up with someone you know."

As his jaw slackened, she knew she'd struck on the truth. And whomever he was confusing her with was someone he didn't like.

"I just wanted to point out that if you have to alter your plans, it won't be the end of the world. Surely your family will understand."

"My plans don't involve my family," she said softly. *Would Chris understand?* she wondered. They'd been planning Thursday's outing for months now. And he liked things to work on schedule. But of course he'd understand. Anyone would. If she called him, he'd probably insist on driving up here to get her himself.

"Sorry," he said through the darkness. "I didn't mean to pry. Listen, you have my word as mayor we'll send you on your way as soon as humanly possible."

He thought he heard her sigh and wondered if it was a sigh of relief. Getting her home right away was best, he reasoned. She interested him more than he wanted anyone to.

"I'll manage to find a way," she insisted politely. Just because she was dazed as a twit when they met, she didn't want him thinking she was a weakling. He'd done much to help her, yet she had the distinct feeling he'd be happy to see her hit the highway.

He smiled to himself. "I'm sure you will. Have you eaten dinner?"

Her stomach responded with a sharp pang.

"I think I missed it," she confessed.

"I just wondered because I was going to stop

and eat after dropping you off, and I know for a fact our hotel doesn't offer room service. It would suit me fine to stop before dropping you off."

"It's fine with me," she answered.

Ben chanced a quick glance at the woman on the seat beside him. He told himself he was just being neighborly to someone in trouble, not wanting to admit the truth that he didn't want to leave her company just yet.

He thought a lot around this time of year about being alone. But he usually dismissed these thoughts as rapidly as they popped into his head.

He turned the car into the parking lot of a steakhouse he knew would still be open.

"There's no point in both of us eating alone tonight anyway," he said quickly as he killed the ignition, getting out of the car before she had time to reply. Almost as if the thought embarrassed him.

Surprised, Sharon realized she agreed with him. Normally, she enjoyed being alone. But after the jarring accident, she found she was in no hurry to be engulfed in a solitary motel room. Tonight, she wanted human companionship and she attributed her need to lingering jitters. Perhaps she would later take the doctor's tranquilizer after all.

By the time she reached for the door handle,

Ben had already rounded the car and was pulling open the door.

"Thanks," she said, catching the tantalizing aroma of good, hot food wafting from the building.

Ben ushered her inside, waving to several seated diners who called out to him and gave her speculative looks.

"They're all staring," she whispered.

"Trying to figure out who you are," he said, keeping his smile in place as he picked up trays and silverware. "I hope you don't mind too much. This is a small town."

Sharon placed a glass of ice water on her tray. "I've wondered sometimes what it was like here."

He turned to her. "Why?"

Sharon shrugged. "My grandfather used to live here. He's dead now."

"You should ask my aunt about him. Maybe she remembers him."

"I will."

She studied the menu, wondering why she was telling him about her grandfather.

After ordering steak and a baked potato, she carried her tray to a booth in the corner. Ben followed.

"Good choice," he noted, arranging his iced tea

oand silverware. "Out of view of curious onlookers."

"A lot of people in this town seem interested in your welfare," she returned.

"Speculating when I'm going to get married again," he said.

She quickly masked the surprise that rose to her expression.

But she couldn't help asking, "Are you divorced?"

"My wife died," he said, and looked out the window.

Sharon wished she hadn't pried. Obviously, she'd revived a painful memory. It was none of her business anyway.

"I shouldn't have asked," she said softly.

"It's all right. It was a long time ago." But his tone warned he didn't want to discuss it further.

Sharon wanted to back off, but she wasn't sure how to change the subject without sounding callous. Silence tumbled through the air like a heavy rain cloud, until it was he who broke it.

"And so?" he asked. "What exactly is it you do for the children's museum?"

"There's little that I don't do," she said, kicking into her public relations spiel lauding the museum programs aimed at interesting youth in art.

"I imagine that's difficult in a world brimming with video games and television," he ventured.

"We don't kid ourselves and pretend those will go away," she explained. "We just want them to see what else is available. The biggest problem is capturing their attention long enough to do that."

Ben admired her obvious dedication. "It must be quite a place."

"It is. And we're lucky to have visiting collections by people like your aunt."

"She'd be proud to hear you say that. Sara has always loved children."

Sharon nodded. "She'd have to, to paint the way she does. Adults like her work too, it brings back something for them, I think."

Ben caught the sparkle in her eyes, and they looked infinitely blue and intelligent. What else would he discover in their depths? he wondered.

Snagged by the intensity of his glance, Sharon could not look away. What was this man thinking about? She saw kindness and something warm and appealing in his face, something she guessed he preferred not to show to the world.

A shadow hovered over the table, and she looked up to see a waitress standing over them with two large metal plates. She'd nearly forgotten her hunger!

The waitress set the plates down and left.

Sharon delved into her food, watching Ben do the same.

For several minutes, they ate in silence.

"I'm glad you suggested this," Sharon said. "I was awfully hungry, and this food is good. I'm starting to feel much better."

Ben smiled, his expression dimming at the sudden blare of a horn in the parking lot. At the second deafening honk, he rose from his seat.

"Excuse me," he said, leaving her gaping bewilderedly as he strode toward the exit.

She strained to see out into the parking lot through the frost-covered window, then gave up and returned her attention to her food. Maybe this too was some small-town ritual, friends blowing their car horns to summon him out to the parking lot.

No, she reasoned. That was a weird explanation. She hoped Ben wasn't mixed up in something he shouldn't be. He was too nice a man to be involved in shady dealings.

But after all, what did she really know about this man she was dining with? Could the car that came careening down the street earlier have been driven by someone trying to hit him?

She knew she was letting her imagination get the best of her. Everyone here seemed to like Ben, including the police and paramedics. And he was Sara Eagleston's nephew. Besides, her instincts told her he was the kind of person who tried to do the right thing. He'd been nothing but considerate to her since the accident.

She continued eating as though nothing unusual had happened. Several minutes later he returned. She avoided looking up as he sat down.

"That was Sara," he announced.

Sharon looked up, puzzled. She set her fork down.

"Why didn't she come inside?" she asked.

To her chagrin, he laughed.

"What's so funny?" she demanded, abandoning her instincts and becoming convinced he was a maniac.

"She was on the phone. My car horn honks if a call comes in and I don't answer."

Sharon's expression slackened with relief. Once she started laughing, she couldn't stop until her sides hurt.

"I couldn't imagine what you were doing out there," she admitted.

"There wasn't time to explain," he apologized, enjoying her hearty laughter.

He waited until she was calm before speaking again. "Sara is terribly upset about the accident and requested I bring you to her house tonight. I told her that was up to you."

Sharon considered. She felt tired and grubby

and disoriented, and mentally she'd already postponed the interview until she felt fresh in the morning.

But Sara Eagleston was much in demand, and the museum needed her more than she needed them. She was doing Sharon a huge favor by consenting to this interview for the exhibit brochure.

If she wanted Sharon's presence tonight, she would have it.

"You don't mind taking me there?" Sharon asked. "You've done so much already."

Ben eyed her evenly. "I don't mind taking you tonight or in the morning. It's up to you when you want to go. My aunt can be unreasonable. I know for a fact she'll be home in the morning."

Sharon shrugged. "I might as well go ahead. That way I'll be ready to leave as soon as my car is repaired."

"All right," Ben agreed, stirring his tea. He hated to see her get her hopes up about the car. "To my aunt's mansion it is."

"Great," Sharon said. Suddenly, she felt a little reckless in this strange town, accompanied by a man whose telephone called him from the parking lot. Just like her habit of buckling her seat belt, she had never realized how well-ordered her life was until now. And she felt a little like she was driving without that protective harness.

The tension between them eased somewhat on the drive to Mrs. Eagleston's house. Like a tour guide, Ben chatted amiably about his hometown, pausing intermittently to point out landmarks. The sound of his voice was soothing, and Sharon remained content to sit inside the darkened car interior and just listen.

Finally, he stopped in the midst of a story about the old library the local citizenry had raised money to save and turned to her. "Are you always this quiet?" he asked. "Or am I monopolizing the conversation? I have a tendency to do that. Bad habit."

Sharon answered with a flounce of her head and smiled slightly. "No, I'm enjoying the guided tour, although I have to admit it's difficult to see much in the dark. Actually, I was mulling things over. I didn't mean to be rude."

"What things?" he asked nonchalantly, as though they had known each other for a long time.

Although Sharon shrank from the personal nature of the question, his casual way of asking kept her from fending him off. And maybe, right now, he was the one person who would understand what she was feeling.

Her voice sounded small and faraway. "About how life and death can be measured in seconds and inches. I suppose it sounds silly talking about it now, since we're both perfectly all right."

Ben tighted his grip on the steering wheel. "It doesn't sound silly at all. I've been thinking about the same thing since the crash. Maybe the problem is that when things like this happen, the people involved go on about their business and don't think or talk about it."

"Maybe it's because dwelling on it could drive a person mad," Sharon suggested, surprised at how natural this discussion seemed.

He glanced sidewise, and even in the darkened car, she felt his eyes on her. Something sparked inside her, startling her with its slow heat and intensity. She'd been aware of Ben's attractiveness since first setting eyes on him earlier, but she hadn't anticipated feeling drawn to him.

That she did made her feel guilty and shocked. She pushed the feelings aside. She and Ben had shared the experience of a narrowly diverted disaster. It was only normal that it would link them, she reasoned. But that was the only bond she had with this man, she reminded herself.

"I believe everything happens for a reason," he stated.

"So do I," she agreed. "There was a reason we escaped serious injury."

He shook his head. "You're seeing it the way you want to see it. What I mean is, there was a reason the accident occured at all."

"Other than that fruitcake flying in out of nowhere, I can't see what."

Ben's eyebrows danced. "Fruitcake?" he chuckled.

"What's so funny about that?"

He rubbed his jaw. "Nothing. I just never heard that word used quite that way before."

Sharon shrugged. "What you were saying is that the accident was fated?"

He grew serious once again. "I don't know. Maybe it's a warning. Food for thought."

"Like we're living bad lives and should change them?"

"Maybe we just need to appreciate our lives more."

"I'm quite grateful for mine without wrecking the car," she offered. But she grasped what he meant, and she knew where it hit home. But she grasped what he meant, and she knew where it hit home. She'd enjoy life more if she could deal with crises better, accept things. For example, her car being disabled was not the end of the world—simply an inconvenience.

She studied his bold profile. "But the fear is humbling," she added.

Ben nodded in agreement, and they both laughed to ward off graver thoughts.

"It makes you think," he said. "About other people. People who aren't as lucky as we are."

Sharon had never considered herself lucky, but since Ben pointed it out, she realized she was. Today at least.

The car smoothed to a stop.

Sharon's head jerked up, and she looked out the window at a brightly lit, columned brick house centered on a sprawling lawn.

"It is a mansion," she observed, unable to mask her awe.

Ben laughed. "Just what a 71-year-old woman needs to live in by herself, don't you think?" he asked.

Sharon gripped the door handle. "You sound as though you disapprove of your aunt."

"Not really. But I do worry about her, living out here alone. Aunt Sara is not a person who listens to reason. Giving the orders is all she knows. I sometimes wonder if something were wrong, whether she'd tell anyone."

"It's good that she's self-sufficient," Sharon noted. "A person who loses her independence loses her self-respect."

Ben's glance beat down on her. "You and Sara should get along fine," he said.

What did I say? she wondered as she stepped out of the car. Then suddenly, she saw Ben in a new light. A male chauvinist. Perhaps he thought only men could look out for themselves. She remembered his earlier comment about her hectic lifestyle.

Well, she was not the complacent, rural woman he was probably used to, content to sit home and milk the cows, letting her husband take credit for it.

"I see," she said bitingly.

Ben swung the door shut, wondering what he'd done to irritate her. Couldn't she understand that an elderly relative living alone would be a constant source of worry to him?

He pushed aside his concern. Sharon would be on her way home in the morning. Did it matter so much what she thought of him?

He followed her up the stone walkway.

"Wait up," he called, surprised when she complied.

As he caught up to her, he couldn't help noticing how pretty she was, how gracefully she moved despite lugging her pocketbook and camera case that hung from straps over her shoulder.

"What is it?" she asked.

Chapter Three

From Ben's description of his great aunt, Sharon expected a grandame in a flowing gown with a great mass of snow white hair coiled in a regal knot over her head.

The oval-faced woman in jeans and denim shirt with short blonde hair and dangling filigree silver earrings who answered the door quickly shattered that image.

"You must be Sharon," the woman greeted her enthusiastically. "From all our lengthy telephone conversations in past weeks, I feel as though I already know you. Please, come on in."

Sharon smiled gratefully and allowed herself to be ushered inside with Ben, exchanging pleasantries with his aunt, trailing behind her. She did feel as though this warm, friendly woman was someone she had already met, or would have liked to.

Sara was short and slightly plump with the appearance of a woman ten years her junior. She led them into a long living room, bright with snow white walls and matching carpeting. The furniture was upholstered in a robin's egg blue, matching the draperies. The end tables were white with glass tops.

A brick fireplace at the far end of the room was adorned with baskets of pine cones and dried autumn foliage. Sharon felt comfortable here immediately. To her, the most stunning aspect of the room was the line of framed oil paintings along the walls, Mrs. Eagleston's creations.

Bigger than life, they featured whimsical saucer-eyed characters with hair as fine as cotton candy and pinkish complexions. Fantasy blended with reality as the pixies pranced across the canvases.

Sharon inspected the pictures. "Your work is wonderful," she said sincerely. She'd believed this since the first time she'd set eyes on any of it and had devoted a lot of hard work to borrowing the older woman's collection for the museum.

These were just the kinds of pieces that would prod an otherwise unresponsive child into a love of art.

"Thank you," Mrs. Eagleston replied without

false modesty. "I would have laughed ten years ago if anyone had told me I could make a good living doing this. It's so much fun, it doesn't feel like work."

"Really?" Sharon asked with uplifted eyebrow. "Surely you must have wanted to take up painting before?"

Sara tossed her blonde hair. "Oh, no, dear," she said earnestly. "Of course I sewed when I was raising my children, but that was about the most artistic of my endeavors. I had no inkling I could do anything like this. I only took an art course to fill the hours after the children were grown and my husband passed on."

Sharon nodded, although she found this difficult to comprehend. Living so many years with such talent and not being aware of it seemed to her like living over an untapped gold mine.

"Sit down," Sara urged. "I'll get us some coffee and be right back."

Sharon dropped onto the sofa as their hostess disappeared around the corner, poignantly aware of Ben sliding onto the cushion beside hers. She turned and looked up at him. He merely smiled.

Finally, he said, "I knew you two would like each other."

"I've admired your aunt's work for a long time."

"No harm in that, but she doesn't let those she's fond of off easily."

Sharon's expression darkened. "What do you mean by that?"

As his mouth dropped open, Sara rounded the corner carrying a silver tray of tiny sandwiches, raw vegetables and sugar coated spritz cookies.

"Anything I can do?" Ben offered.

"The coffee's on another tray on the kitchen counter," his great aunt informed him.

Sharon eyed the food warily, thinking of the meal she'd just eaten.

"Oh, I know you two just ate, but the food at that steak house isn't the most satisfying. Just a snack in case you're still hungry."

Sharon didn't think she was, but she politely selected a carrot stick. Ben returned, setting the coffee tray on the table. He filled the three cups from the carafe, then took his and reclaimed his seat.

"I think Sharon's awfully tired tonight, Sara," he told his aunt. "The accident was unnerving for all of us."

Sara's alert blue eyes flickered. "Yes, and I'm glad to see you're both unharmed. I do thank you for bringing her here, Ben. I should have considered the holiday traffic, Sharon. We could have postponed the interview until next weekend."

"I'm taking a trip this weekend," Sharon explained. "I'd hoped to have the article for the brochure completed before Thanksgiving."

Sara shook her head then looked down into her coffee cup. "I guess I should have just sent you some of those press releases I have."

"Mrs. Eagleston, I would have come to take the photographs anyway. And I wanted to meet you. You're not responsible for my accident. It was just..." She groped for a word. "Fate."

She felt Ben's elbow nudge hers.

Why did she have this constant feeling he was making fun of her?

She shot him a warning glance, and he feigned innocence.

"Is something wrong?" Sara asked, her eyes swinging between the two of them.

"No," Sharon insisted quickly, reaching for a sandwich. She bit into it, delighted by the unexpected flavor of seasoned cream cheese topped by a single slice of wafer-thin roast beef.

"My aunt," Ben announced, catching Sharon's approving look, "has always been famous for her cooking. Long before her artistic talents were discovered." He captured one of the sandwiches in his large hand.

"I enjoy having visitors to cook for," Sara admitted, tossing Ben an accusing glance.

"And it's always worth the trip out here," Ben added, ignoring her piercing look.

Agreeing, Sharon helped herself to another of the irresistible sandwiches. She took one bite, then sat the remainder on a napkin while she fished in her pocketbook for a notebook and pen.

"I suppose we should go ahead and start on the interview," she suggested, acknowledging, "I have had an incredibly long day." While she appreciated Ben's speaking up on her behalf earlier, she believed in speaking up for herself.

Sara Eagleston motioned for her to put the pad and pen away. "I wouldn't hold you to our original appointment time."

"But..." Sharon began, puzzled as to why Sara had summoned them here tonight.

"But I can't think of you staying in our pitiful little hotel after what you've been through, and not having any transportation. You'll stay here tonight, of course."

Sharon's lips rounded in astonishment. Now she understood what Ben had meant about his aunt being someone you didn't say no to. "I couldn't..." she faltered.

"Of course you can. Goodness knows I've got plenty of room. You'll be much more comfortable here, and it will make me feel better."

Sharon's eyes shifted momentarily to Ben. What is it with this family?

Ben smiled softly. He knew Sharon wouldn't refuse now.

"I'll get your things from the car," he offered generously.

Helplessly, Sharon watched him go.

Sara Eagleston tucked one leg beneath her and hugged one knee. "And you can fill me in on what's going on in the mysterious world of art. I stay cooped up here most of the time."

Sharon realized her initial reservations stemmed from unfamiliarity with such immediate and overwhelming generosity. Doubtless, this house would be more comfortable than a motel room. And she would have a chance to really get to know Sara. It would help her with her work. The invitation was a touching gesture.

Ben returned quickly with her meager luggage and carried it upstairs for her. When he came down, he moved to leave, and once again, Sharon was filled with an inexplicable reluctance to see him go.

"Thank you," she said. How inadequate the words seemed considering all he'd done. "Please take your coat." She pressed it into his arms.

He tipped his hat. "I'll see you in the morning."

Sharon's expression went blank.

"You'll want to see about your car," he reminded her.

"Of course," she said, relieved at the knowledge she'd be seeing him again. How could she have forgotten so quickly about her poor car? Just hours ago its condition had seemed a matter of life and death.

Sara insisted Sharon make free use of her telephone to call her family or whomever she needed to notify of her whereabouts. Now, alone in the bedroom with the telephone, she reluctantly dialed Chris's number.

After five rings, his answering machine clicked on. She almost hung up without leaving a message, realizing how garbled a two-minute explanation of what had happened would sound. But she did need to alert him that her arrival back in Pensacola might be delayed, so she conveyed that and left Sara's number.

Setting the receiver back in its cradle, she scanned the room that looked like something from a house and garden magazine with its splashy floral prints and canopied bed. Sara Eagleston obviously liked nice things, and Sharon admired her taste.

She switched off the lamp and shimmied down beneath crisp lace-trimmed linen sheets and a fluffy comforter. The bed was soft, warm, and cozy, and feeling pampered, she relaxed. She'd definitely have no need for the doctor's tranquilizer tonight.

As she began drifting off, she thought not of Chris, but of Ben with his kindness and his oddly annoying sense of humor. This whole episode, she thought, was like a dream, and he was a part of it.

And in her muddied thoughts, she tried to warn herself not to make too much of it, because in the light of day there would be real life to face once again.

"This house has been in my husband's family for years," Sara explained over waffles dusted with powdered sugar the next morning. She and Sharon sat face-to-face in a sunlit corner of her black-and-white tiled kitchen.

Sharon sipped her coffee. "It's very impressive," she noted.

Sara laughed gleefully. "I really don't give a hoot about dazzling anyone. The place would be falling down around my feet if it wasn't for my painting. The money enabled me to do some remodeling. I've fixed it just the way I like it."

"You must enjoy it very much."

A shadow crossed Mrs. Eagleston's sunny face. "I just wish it could have been this nice when my family was here to enjoy it, especially my husband. But when you're busy with a family, you have other priorities. Keeping the children in clean underwear is more important than buying new curtains to match the bedspread."

She smiled softly, and Sharon realized she must be thinking about the days when this house bustled with young children. The cheerfulness reflected in her paintings must stem from those days, she thought.

"How many children do you have?" Sharon asked.

"Two daughters and two sons. They all married and moved away to larger cities years ago, and of course some of my grandchildren are married now as well. We all try to get together sometime between Thanksgiving and Christmas. It's just impossible for everyone to come on a holiday."

"It sounds like quite a crowd," Sharon noted, thinking of her own splintered family that never gathered together.

"Oh yes, we have a wonderful time. What about you? Is your family planning a big Thanksgiving dinner?"

Sharon suspected the woman must have been reading her thoughts.

"No," she conceded. "My parents died a long time ago. My aunt and uncle raised me and my older sister, and they live in New Mexico now.

My sister's busy with her own family. My boyfriend and I are planning to have dinner with his parents."

"That sounds serious," Mrs. Eagleston commented with keen interest.

"I expect we'll be getting engaged, probably at Christmas," Sharon said slowly. She wondered at her own lack of enthusiasm. She longed for a home and a family, and she knew Chris wanted the same things. Still, now that it was going to happen, she had a nagging sense of being unprepared.

"Well, I wish my nephew Ben would find someone like you. That boy's had a hard time of it since his wife died. Hasn't given anyone a second look."

"Maybe he hasn't gotten over her," Sharon suggested.

Sara shook her head. "Not likely. From what I saw, it wasn't a happy marriage. She was a retailer from Atlanta, and she wasn't interested in staying home and having children."

"Lots of women today balance careers and families. Staying home is a luxury."

But Sara was adamant. "Ben makes a good living. She was just more in love with her job than with him."

"You didn't like her," Sharon said.

Sara paled guiltily. "I tried to, really. It's just

that Ben seemed so unhappy so often. He's always been special, and she kept trying to persuade him to move to Atlanta. I know he would have been miserable in all that congestion."

Sharon swallowed hard, trying to stifle her curiousity about Ben. She felt as though she were tresspassing, hearing all the private details of his life. After all, they were merely acquaintances.

"I do love having Ben living nearby," Sara continued. "But we don't see eye-to-eye on what my needs are. He thinks of me as an eccentric, frail old woman who needs constant looking after and should be living in town in a dreary retirement home. I just like to have him visit. Perhaps if he had a family of his own, he'd ease off."

Sharon couldn't resist her deep desire to know what had happened to Ben. "How did his wife die?" she asked.

But before Sara could answer, she was interrupted by the shrill ringing of the telephone.

"Excuse me," she said, as she rose to answer it. There was an extension right there on the kitchen wall.

"Hello," Sara answered brightly, then a few seconds later extended the receiver. "It's for you."

Sharon remembered the message she'd left on Chris's machine last night.

She took the receiver eagerly.

"Chris?"

But it wasn't his voice she heard. "No, this is Ben. Are you ready to go into town and see about your car?"

She struggled to hide the disappointment and embarrassment that crept into her voice. "Oh, yes, thank you. Your aunt and I were just having breakfast."

"Good, save me some waffles."

"How did you know we were having waffles?"

"Sara always makes them for company. I'll be there in a few minutes."

"Thank you, bye."

As she hung up, she glanced at the clock on the wall. It was nearly ten. She and Sara had indulged in a leisurely breakfast. Surely Chris should have called by now.

"Ben's on his way," Sharon announced, turning to Sara.

"Do you want to try to call your friend again?" the artist offered, refilling their coffee cups.

Sharon shook her head. After all, she hadn't explained her predicament to Chris, only that she'd been delayed getting back. He probably assumed the interview was more involved than she'd thought and saw no need to call.

But she'd left the number. Why else would she have done that if she didn't need to speak to him? One of the shrewdest young attorneys in Florida could have easily figured that out. Wasn't he even curious about the delay?

She pushed her irritation aside. Her disrupted plans had frayed her nerves, causing her to overreact. She merely wanted to complete her work so she could resume her normal life.

Returning to the table, she sipped her hot coffee and told Sara, "Since Ben's coming to take me to the garage, I suppose I should contact the insurance company. Can we do the interview when I get back?"

Sara nodded in agreement. "That will be fine. I'll bake my pies for tomorrow while you're gone."

As if on cue, the phone rang again. Sara answered it, once again handing the receiver to Sharon. "I believe it is your beau this time, dear," she whispered.

Relieved, Sharon smiled slightly as she went to the phone. Sara had emerged from a much more romantic world than she lived in—"Beau."

She smiled as she took the receiver. "Chris?" Her voice echoed like she was talking into a tin can, and she knew he'd put her on the speaker phone in his office.

"What's the problem?" His down-to-business attorney's voice came over the line.

It brought a touch of reality to her situation, and she was glad to hear it. She related the details of the accident.

"When will you be getting back?" he asked.

Her heart dropped a little as she picked up the irritation in his voice. He could have shown, she thought, a little more concern. But she reminded herself Chris wasn't a person who showed his feelings easily.

"Late tonight, I hope. We're going to check on my car in a few minutes. I'll have to call you back later."

"I'll probably be in court the rest of the day. Leave a message with Bernice, okay?"

"Sure."

The doorbell rang. Sara disappeared from the kitchen.

"I guess I'll see you in the morning," she added, preparing to end the conversation.

"Oh, Sharon..."

Her spirits lifted. "Yes?"

"Have you thought any more about applying for Millicent's position?"

The warmth in her heart evaporated. "No," she answered.

"You can't wait much longer, you know."

Her eyes widened as Ben's smiling figure filled

the door frame. He was dressed in jeans and a blue and red flannel shirt. He looked, she thought, even more handsome in the daylight. His dancing eyes seemed to be drinking her in, and as they caught hers, a strange but pleasant fever coursed through her.

"Sharon?"

Guiltily, she remembered Chris. "Yes, I know, Chris. We can talk about it tomorrow."

"I'll see you then. And be careful driving home."

"Bye." She refrained from pointing out the accident wasn't the result of her carelessness.

Ben was seated at his aunt's table, attacking a stack of waffles. "Letting everyone know you're safe and sound?" he asked.

"Yes," Sharon lied, trying not to dwell on the fact that Chris hadn't inquired about her well-being. Well, she reasoned, he knew she could take care of herself. At least he had confidence in her.

She finished her coffee while Ben ate then helped Sara rinse dishes and load them in the dishwasher. She phoned her insurance company and was told the person who handled her account wouldn't be in until Monday.

As she and Ben walked out to his car, she told him, "I appreciate your taking time off work to help me with this."

"No problem, the plant practically runs itself, for short periods of time, anyway. But this is our busy season."

Her brow furrowed as she turned to look at him. "What kind of business are you in?"

"Fruitcake," he announced proudly, adding a deep laugh when he saw her astonished expression.

"Fruitcake?" she repeated.

"As gifts. We have a few other products too, gourmet desserts. But we're famous for 'Russell's Fruitcakes.' Haven't you heard of them?"

"I don't eat much fruitcake. I didn't think anyone really ate them."

"Well, that's because you've never tried ours. I assure you, it's different. A secret family recipe."

She lifted one eyebrow. "Sounds intriguing," she answered.

Her face was red from the cold, and a sudden gust of wind blew her hair into a streamer behind her. Ben looked down on her, overwhelmed with a surge of unexpected affection.

"Good," he said. "I'd like nothing better than to intrigue you."

Taken aback by his comment, Sharon paused mid-stride, her eyes shooting up to meet his. His eyes held hers for a long moment, searching for an explanation. Uncomfortable with the inten-

sity of the encounter, she just as quickly tore
her eyes away and resumed her pace.

He was toying with her, she concluded, fearing he sensed her fierce, unwanted fascination
with him.

Ben, racing to keep up with her, mentally
kicked himself for letting the remark slip out.
A stranger inside him had said it, but the truth
was he meant it. He'd been thinking about her
ever since last night.

Now she probably thought he was the local
Don Juan, and he had no desire to make her
uncomfortable in his presence, especially since
he enjoyed being with her and could talk to her
so easily.

She reached the car, opened the unlocked passenger door, and climbed inside. Ben got in the
driver's side.

"I would have opened the door for you, if you'd
waited," he said.

"No need," she protested. "I'm used to opening
doors for myself."

"Sorry. I wouldn't want my manners to usurp
your independence."

Sharon lowered her eyes. "I've learned not to
count on anyone else to do things for me. I don't
know if you can understand that, you seem to
be surrounded by family and friends. It hasn't

always been that way for me. I don't mean to be rude."

"But you are upset because of what I said out there on the sidewalk."

She stared at the dashboard, not answering.

"All I meant," he defended himself, "was that I like you. Maybe it came out wrong."

She looked up at him. "You seem to be a kind, warm-hearted man, although somewhat impossible. I can see why everyone here likes you so much, enough to elect you mayor. And you've certainly gone out of your way to help me, a complete stranger. I don't see how anyone could not like you."

Finding her answer evasive, he settled for it, gunning the motor. After all, she was anxious to be on her way home and once she left chances were slim that their paths would ever cross again. Better to leave things as they were.

A short way up the road, Sharon burst into a gale of laughter.

"What is it?" he asked.

"No wonder you reacted so strangely when I called that other driver a fruitcake last night."

Ben joined her laughter.

The shared joke chipped away at the tension between them. Sharon sat back enjoying the scenery the small town offered, houses perched on hillsides, antique stores in old houses trimmed with gingerbread, a tiny grocery store and gas station that looked like relics from the 1950s.

She regretted the ride ended so soon, as Ben pulled the car into the mechanic's shop. He introduced her to Mr. Towers, who delivered the bad news about her car. He estimated two weeks to fix the body.

"Can't you just do enough work to make it drivable?" she implored.

The thin man shook his head. "No way. Can't even get started until your insurance adjuster gets here." He took her to the car, which looked even worse to her in the daylight, and detailed what had to be done.

Sharon nodded gravely. "Where can I get a rental car? I have to be back in Pensacola by tonight."

"Vernon Smith has some cars. You might try him," the man suggested.

Although Sharon hated the prospect of leaving her car here, she felt she didn't have a choice.

"Can I use your phone?" Ben asked.

"Sure, Ben," the man said easily. Sharon felt sure if Ben had asked to borrow a thousand dollars the answer would have been the same. What was it about this man that had everybody in such a trance?

Ben ushered her inside the shop's office.

Sharon looked around at the accumulated dust and grit and random piles of papers on the disorderly desk. The orange flame of a space heater glowed in one corner. She stuck her hands in the pocket of her wool coat and tapped her foot on the concrete floor.

Ben's expression was grim when he hung up the phone and turned to her. "He only has three cars, and none are due back before Monday."

"Three cars?" Sharon asked incredulously.

"The rentals are just a sideline. His business is selling used cars."

Her expression dropped. "I suppose I'll have to check the bus schedules."

"We can call back at Sara's house," Ben assured her.

Sharon nodded. She thanked Mr. Towers and went with Ben back to his car.

"You know," Ben said slowly. "The plant's closed tomorrow. I could drive you back to Pensacola."

Her eyes widened at the magnitude of his suggestion. "And give up your holiday? And have to drive all the way back? No, I draw the line there, Ben. I can't let you do that. Besides, it's imperative I reach home tonight."

He looked at her long and hard, but didn't say anything.

Suddenly, his car phone rang, startling Sharon who had forgotten about the device.

He picked up the receiver with one hand. "Hello?"

After several seconds of silence, he said, "I'll be right there."

"Is everything all right?" Sharon asked.

He nodded. "I'm afraid we'll have to stop by the plant if you don't mind. It's no major crisis, but a major customer has stopped by and is waiting to see me in person. He's head of a company that purchases our fruitcakes for each of its employees every year." His tone was almost apologetic.

"I don't mind," she assured him. "I'd love to see where fruitcakes come from."

"I can do better than that. I'll give you a sample."

She grimaced.

"I saw that," he noted.

Sharon smiled. A lovely smile, he couldn't help thinking. Too bad she wasn't the kind of person who would ever stay here. He'd learned that lesson too hard once before.

"I'll try to keep an open mind."

"You know in the old days people would make their fruitcakes in the fall, douse them with booze, wrap them in cloth, and leave them on the back porch to age."

"Are yours doused in booze?"

He shook his head. "Strictly nonalcoholic. But I kind of like the tradition. Making something so far in advance and saving it for a special day. Everyone today wants everything right away."

Sharon reflected on her impatience about her car.

"It's a faster moving world today. I'd lay odds you don't age your fruitcakes either."

"You've got me there. Don't get me wrong, I'm not living in the past. I just think it's worth looking back on sometimes."

"All we have is the present," she said.

"Which diminishes without the past and the future."

"Maybe for you." She straightened her rose-colored sweater. "For some of us it's easier to concentrate on the here and now."

Ben's sheltering instincts shifted into gear. What had happened to her that made her want to obliterate the past? Still, he fought to mask the swelling protectiveness he felt toward her, fearing it would result in another slip, another comment or action that would make her think he was getting too close.

"What about art?" he asked. "Isn't that part of history?"

"I prefer modern art."

He shook his head. Despite all her poise and

control, he believed this young woman was running from something that frightened her. Or maybe she was just running from him.

And as he pulled into his reserved parking space in front of his plant, he wished more than anything for a chance to find out.

Chapter Four

Sharon sat on the long leather sofa in Ben's outer office, inspecting the polished pine paneling and listening to the soft murmur of piped-in music. A nice, comfortable atmosphere, she reflected.

"Could I get you some coffee or a soft drink?" Ben's secretary, Glynis Bright, who sat at a desk opposite her, offered.

Sharon smiled at the dark-haired woman. "No, thank you. I'm fine. Don't let me keep you from your work."

"Nonsense," Glynis insisted. "I was just going to get a cup for myself anyway. How do you take it, black or with cream and sugar?"

"Cream and sugar," Sharon gave in.

When Glynis rose from behind the desk, Sharon was surprised to see she wore blue jeans with her plaid sweater and ornate jewelry.

"It's a dress-down day," Glynis explained, catching Sharon's expression. "We have them every Friday, and today because it's the day before a holiday. Ben believes comfortable employees are more productive. I must admit, it seems effective. I wouldn't work for anyone else."

She set off down the hall. Ben Russell, Sharon considered, was a very smart man. She smoothed the legs of her own blue jeans, no longer self-conscious about wearing them in an office building. But then, Ben himself had come dressed equally as casual to greet a client.

Glynis returned momentarily, bearing a steaming styrofoam cup in each hand. She handed one to Sharon, then sat at her desk, sipping the hot liquid. She shook her head. "Yes, when I worked in the city, I had some bosses that were real killers."

"You moved here from the city?" Sharon asked incredulously.

"About three years ago, after I found this job. I'm divorced, and I found Atlanta was no place to try raising two sons alone. Here, it's almost like the whole town is family."

"Isn't it a little too quiet?" Sharon asked.

Glynis shrugged. "Sometimes, but the benefits outweigh the disadvantages. I miss the stores and the shows and museums, but it's not that far to drive in to Atlanta for all that." She glanced at her watch. "I hope Ben won't be tied up too long. I hated cutting short your outing. If Ben would just quit trying to do all the marketing along with everything else on his own, he wouldn't have this many demands on his time."

"Oh, it wasn't an outing really. Ben just took me to the garage to see about my car. Do customers drop by like this all the time?"

"It's not unusual. Things are real informal. Most of our business is by mail order or through some distributors. The company's grown a lot in the last few years. People who thought they didn't like fruitcake are discovering ours."

The corners of Sharon's lips turned upward as she remembered Ben had boasted the same thing. She was going to have to taste this stuff.

"Ben says it's an old family recipe."

"Yes, it was developed by Ben's grandfather, Timothy Russell, and his partner, Devan Thomas."

Sharon blanched, her mouth dropping open.

"What's wrong?" Glynis asked.

Sharon absently combed fingers through her hair. "Oh, nothing," she said quickly. Devan was such an unusual name. It was highly unlikely there could have been two Devan Thomases in a small town like this. "What became of Mr. Thomas?"

"I don't really know. He and Mr. Russell had some kind of falling out, and I guess he sold out to Ben's grandfather. Of course, they're both dead now." Glynis flashed an apologetic smile and returned her attention to her coffee.

Sharon burned with curiosity, but she didn't ask any more questions, since Glynis obviously didn't have the answers. An inner voice told her to leave it alone. What difference did an old partnership between her grandfather and Ben's grandfather make?

But she couldn't help glancing around this office, inhaling the aroma of cinnamon and nutmeg drifting in from the bakery, and wondering whether this was part of her heritage. The idea was new to her. She'd been too young when her parents died to have gained much information about her mother's side of the family.

As much as she tried to extinguish the flame, a strange excitement and curiosity filled her.

Glynis didn't have the answers, but Ben might.

She picked up a copy of the company's gift catalog from the end table and thumbed through it, not wanting Glynis to feel obligated to keep her occupied. Glynis returned to her work at the computer terminal, leaving Sharon to her own thoughts.

She was about halfway through the catalog when the door to Ben's office opened, and he emerged with a heavy-set man dressed in khaki. They strolled over to her, and Ben introduced his customer.

Sharon had never heard of him, but she did recognize the name of the company he headed.

After he left, Ben explained, "He was out this way on a hunting trip and decided to stop in and place his holiday order. I'm sorry for the delay." His eyes swung to her coffee on the end table. "I see Glynis took good care of you."

"The mothering instinct," Glynis chimed in without missing a keystroke. "I hope you're planning a tour for Miss Hunicutt before she leaves."

Ben's eyes turned questioningly to Sharon, who had the distinct feeling Glynis, for some reason, was set on keeping her and Ben together. "How about it?" Ben asked. "You don't have to if you're in a hurry to get back to Sara's."

Sharon shrugged. Suddenly, she had all the time in the world—someplace to go, but no way to get there. And she was very interested in seeing this operation her grandfather had helped established.

"Sure," she answered, looking up into Ben's handsome face. "I'd love to see it."

"Settled," he proclaimed, turning once again to Glynis. "Glynis, would you mind calling the bus station and finding out what time Miss Hunicutt can catch a bus to Pensacola?"

Glynis's green eyes flared. She looked at Sharon. "You're not taking the bus all the way back to Florida?" she inquired.

"I'm afraid it's the only way. My car is wrecked."

"And she won't let me drive her," Ben added.

"I couldn't impose like that," Sharon insisted once again.

Ben led her on a tour of the factory. Sharon admired the casual way he greeted his employees, calling each one by name. His presence didn't create any tension, and they all continued about their work. As he introduced them, he described their jobs as though the entire operation depended upon each one's good work. By the time they were through, Sharon understood how he had captured his employees' unyielding loyalty.

They ended the tour with a stop in the small shop at the side of the building, where Ben sliced off a piece of the fruitcake set out on the counter to provide samples. He handed her a thick wedge on a napkin.

"And now," he announced. "The moment of truth. You'll never again say you don't like fruit-cake."

Obediently, she tasted it, prepared to say she liked it even if it tasted like shoe leather, after Ben had been so kind. But she was not ready for the mild blend of spice and a faint caramel un-dertaste with pecans and cherries and citrus.

Ben watched her face light up with unex-pected delight. He wished he could preserve that look forever.

"Your grandfather's recipe?" she asked.

"No. My grandfather was a businessman. Ac-tually, the recipe originated with his partner."

"Devan Thomas."

"Yes." His eyes narrowed. "How did you know that?"

"Glynis mentioned his name."

Sharon looked up at Ben. She wondered what his reaction would be to the news that her grand-father's former partner was her grandfather. Never well-practiced at skirting the truth, she decided she had to tell him.

"Ben, he was my grandfather."

Ben involuntarily took a step backward, as though he'd seen a ghost. The woman working behind the counter looked up and glanced in their direction.

"You're sure?"

She nodded. "How many Devan Thomases could have lived here? I didn't know anything about this business. I was here when I was a little girl. My grandfather, I barely remember him, ran a restaurant. I remember eating a banana cream pie that tasted like heaven."

Ben was grinning broadly. "I scarfed up many a slice of that pie and other delights from your grandfather's place when I was a boy." His smile faded. "When his wife died, it was like the heart just drained out of him. He boarded the place up and gave away everything inside. How come your parents never came back?"

"They were killed, both of them, in an accident. It must have been right before my grandfather died. Poor Grandpa, losing a daughter, a son-in-law and his wife. No wonder his stamina gave out. My aunt and uncle—my father's sister and her husband—were trying to raise me and my sister along with their own three children. They told us about our grandmother's death, of course, but I guess bringing us here to the funeral would have been too much to manage."

Sharon paused, astonished at how all this poured out. She remembered more about those times than she'd believed she did. Until now, she'd never discussed them, not even with her sister. Some memories were best left locked away.

Ben studied her, seeing through the anxious career woman to the small girl who'd been left orphaned, overwhelmed by the sudden transition to a large family that was not her own. No wonder she preferred not to dwell on the past.

He thought of Devan Thomas, who long ago had always had an errand Ben could run in return for a piece of pie and glass of milk. He'd liked the old man, whose easy nature had contrasted sharply with that of Ben's own stern old grandfather. And now he found himself liking Devan's granddaughter far more than he should.

"Your grandfather was a nice man. I was surprised when he agreed to the partnership with my grandfather. I was too young to really understand what was going on, but I suspect my grandfather wanted Devan's recipes and wouldn't leave him alone until he gave in. My grandfather could be very persuasive."

"But they didn't remain partners."

"No, a few years after the business got off the ground, the partnership was dissolved. I'm not sure of the circumstances, but I know the two of them never got along well. There were a lot of arguments."

She thought of the thick folder of documents a lawyer's office had delivered to her after tracking her down a few years ago, after her grandfather had died. None of them had made any sense to her, and she'd stowed them away on a high shelf in the closet.

She understood her relatives had done the best they could for her and her sister, but she felt in her heart they'd deprived her of having known her grandfather just because it was inconvenient. But then, her grandfather had never made any attempt to contact her. That hurt equally, perhaps more.

"I'll go through the old records," Ben promised. "I want to make sure your grandfather got a fair deal. This company wouldn't exist today if it hadn't been for him."

"No!" Sharon blurted with an intensity that shocked even her. "Both our grandfathers are dead. Let it rest. It doesn't make any difference."

But it did to Ben. He didn't want to live with the knowledge that his livelihood today stemmed from his grandfather having taken advantage of a grief-stricken culinary genius, a maneuver that was not beyond him.

And despite Sharon's protests, she deserved to know what had happened. He wanted to do this for her. After all, she couldn't stop him from going through his own records.

"Isn't it amazing?" he asked. "To find our own pasts so closely linked?"

Sharon shook her head. "I don't care about the past. I shouldn't have told you about my grandfather." But even as she said it, she was appraising her surroundings, trying to imagine the shadowy bearded figure she remembered from her childhood walking through these rooms.

"I'm glad you did," Ben said, tossing an arm around her shoulders. "Thanks, Rhea," he called to his employee behind the counter as he guided Sharon out into the hallway.

A ripple of warmth crept up her spine at the unexpected closeness. It felt nice to be cradled here in the nook of Ben's arm. She felt the heat of his chest through his shirt and inhaled the enticing outdoor scent of him.

She felt as though she could stay here forever.

Ben suddenly halted. He leaned down, his eyes probing hers. She felt small and soft against him. Her eyes widened, leaving him wishing he could read further into their depths. He surveyed her prim narrow mouth, deep pink this morning without benefit of the lipstick she'd been wearing yesterday.

The impulse to kiss her was overwhelming.

Her lips parted slightly as though she were reading his mind.

Would she allow him in that close? he wondered, hoping she would.

But swiftly, he remembered her reaction to

his earlier comment about intriguing her, and he was afraid if he kissed her he'd scare her away forever. No, not now. As much as he wanted to, he couldn't.

Abruptly, he released her, stepping back. He cleared his throat. "Let's go see if Glynis made that phone call," he suggested.

Aware of what had almost happened, aware of how she had longed for it to happen, Sharon attempted to regain her composure. Why had he drawn away, she wondered? Had he suddenly realized he didn't like her all that much?

Acknowledging she would have welcomed his kiss, she knew it was for the best this hadn't actually taken place. She'd soon be on her way home, out of his life forever. But she also knew her life would never be quite the same. She couldn't go home and in good conscience marry Chris as she had planned. Not when this man so easily set off sparks inside her. Clearly, she wasn't capable of making the kind of commitment marriage required.

Chapter Five

When Glynis looked up from her work to see her boss and Sharon Hunicutt re-enter the office, she immediately noticed their strained expressions and wondered what was wrong. It was as if they already knew about the bad news she had to deliver.

In her mind though, the situation wasn't such a tragedy. She'd known Ben Russell for the past three years and had never seen him look at anyone the way he looked at Sharon, like she was a tempting pastry he was eyeing through a bakery case and trying to persuade himself not to buy.

Glynis believed Ben deserved some happiness—lots of it in fact—and she hoped Sharon would stay long enough for him to stop trying to talk himself out of whatever it was he was feeling for her.

71

She admonished herself to mind her own business. But it was difficult. She couldn't bear seeing anyone close to her unhappy, especially someone she thought as highly of as she did Ben.

"Back already?" she asked, trying to lighten the gloomy atmosphere that had blown in the door with them.

"You called the bus station?" he asked.

His tone stabbed at Sharon's heart. He was anxious for her to leave, she surmised. She'd done nothing but cause trouble for him. Still, she knew he'd wanted to kiss her just moments ago.

How could two people who scarcely knew each other have so much electricity between them so quickly? she wondered. It wasn't possible, yet the sparks undeniably existed. Sparks Chris, a man she'd spent much time cautiously getting to know, had never ignited.

No wonder Ben wanted her gone. The entire situation was absurd. Any rational person could see that.

Glynis looked up and emitted a long sigh. "I'm afraid the only bus headed through here for Florida stopped at seven A.M. There's another tomorrow, but surely you don't want to spend Thanksgiving on a bus."

Sharon clasped one hand to a forehead that suddenly felt as though an arrow had been shot through it. Why was it so impossible to leave this town?

She looked up with new hope as Glynis's voice continued. "I did have another idea, and I called the airlines in Atlanta. All today's flights are booked solid, but I did manage to get you a reservation on a flight that leaves tomorrow at eight."

Sharon brightened. Maybe she'd miss the trip to Chris's parent's house, but she and Chris would at least be able to have a holiday dinner together, even if it was in a restaurant.

"You're a genius, Glynis." Sharon praised her.

As Ben watched the soft contours of Sharon's face grow flushed and animated, something inside him grew cold and leaden. Well, of course, he'd known all along she was anxious to get back home. And of course a woman this beautiful had someone waiting for her. He couldn't expect her to want to stay here among strangers and had no right to selfishly want her here.

He thought back to last night, how he'd been feeling down about the holiday. In business and public life he was a success, yet his private life had never been on track. He was nearly thirty years old, and he wanted someone to share his life with and a houseful of children to come home to.

Had he wanted that so much that he'd too

quickly married the wrong woman? Yvonne had cared little about celebrating holidays. To her, they'd been an unpleasant disruption of her work.

Ben had slowly begun discovering he and Yvonne didn't have what it took to build a happy life together. But just as he'd come to that realization and wondered what to do about it, doing nothing really, Yvonne had been killed.

And he'd suffered overwhelming guilt for her death, for the failings of their marriage. He always remembered he'd thought he loved her once and ultimately made her unhappy.

Yes, last night he'd been looking forward to a bleak and lonely holiday. The collision had just been more of his bad luck, he'd thought. Then he'd found Sharon, and his heart had beat a little faster and he'd focused his thoughts on her. He'd believed that was why he felt better when he was around her.

But in the hallway, he'd learned the truth. His feelings for Sharon ran much deeper than being neighborly and assisting a stranded traveler. He'd barely been able to resist kissing her.

But he and Sharon were from two different planets. He wouldn't be responsible for trying to cage another bird and watching it die.

He wanted Sharon to stay here indefinitely, yet he knew the best thing for everyone was for her to leave as soon as possible. He knew what his selfishness could cost others.

He stuffed his hands in the pockets of his jacket and rocked back on his heels. He turned to Sharon, trying not to dwell on the exquisite silver flecks in her eyes, or the regal high cheekbones or the soft slope of her mouth.

"I wouldn't mind getting up early to drive you to Hartsfield," he volunteered.

Her eyes darkened slightly. "Thank you," she said, her gaze directly on him. "I'm sure it will be a relief to have me finally out of your hair for good."

Just as Ben was about to protest, despite his better judgment, that that was the last thing he really wanted, Glynis cut into their conversation.

"Whoa!" she said, waving a slip of notepaper in the air. "I'm afraid no one's going to have to get up early. The flight leaves at eight P.M. I'm sorry, Sharon, it was the best I could do."

Sharon's eyes fell. She felt the heat of Ben's gaze on her, and when she lifted her eyes to meet his, she had the funniest sensation. Oddly enough, some traitorous part of her looked into that devilishly handsome face and rejoiced at the prospect of lingering in his presence. But odder still, she sensed Ben was feeling the same thing.

She chalked it up to her imagination. Hadn't he just a few minutes ago been inquiring about bus schedules with a brisk impatience?

"It's not your fault," she assured the secretary. "I should have known this was going to happen."

Ben eyed her sympathetically. "Sara will love having the extra company for dinner," he offered.

"I'll just be in the way. Maybe I should move to the hotel."

"Sara won't allow that, and neither will I. I'm going over there for dinner anyway. After we eat, I'll drive you to Atlanta. It's the best I can do."

Sharon's eyes shot up to meet his. "You're not obligated, you know. Neither is Sara. This is my problem."

Ben shook his head. "Come on. Let's go tell Sara. Your bad news will make her day."

Sharon bade Glynis good-bye and thanked her for her help.

Once they were out in the parking lot, Ben turned to her and said, "Why is it so difficult for you to accept help from anyone?"

He'd anticipated her response to be angry, defensive, but instead she replied thoughtfully. "Until I'd finished college and started working at the museum, I was always a burden to someone. My aunt did the best she could for me and my sister. I know it wasn't easy. She never complained in front of us, but I heard her at night, talking to my uncle about how hard life was with two extra children in the house. And my sister postponed her marriage while she was working to put me through college. I promised myself never to be a hardship to anyone again."

Sympathy churned inside him as he looked down on this suddenly fragile, slim woman. His heart ached for her.

"I promise," he said. "I'm never going to complain about your being here, and neither is Sara. We don't operate that way. In fact, the two of us trying to eat the entire turkey Sara insists on cooking every year is a pretty boring prospect. Having you here has brightened the holiday for both of us, for me especially."

Sharon's face turned crimson at his last remark.

"You have a gift for flattery," she proposed.

"No," he retorted. "Ask anyone in town. When I say something I mean it. That's why I'm mayor. Look, Thanksgiving wasn't exactly an event I was looking forward to, except for the chance to spend some time with Sara, who thinks I don't do nearly enough of that. She's the only family I have left here in town, and in the midst of the company's busy season, I don't have time to travel to visit either of my parents or other relatives."

"Your parents have moved away?"

"They're divorced. My dad was running the fruitcake business for a while, before the marriage broke up and he remarried and moved to California. That's why I moved back here from Atlanta to take over. I couldn't stand the thought of the company being sold to outsiders or closed down and the town losing so many jobs."

"Atlanta," she said. "That's where you met your wife?"

"Yes. I guess I never realized how ill-suited we were until we came here. She never did feel comfortable here."

Sharon wondered how anyone could feel unwelcome in such a beautiful place, married to such a warm, generous man.

She reminded herself she knew so little about him. Perhaps there was another side to him she hadn't seen.

"Do you miss her?" she asked.

"She was a lovely, vibrant woman. Even if she had survived, our marriage wouldn't have. But she was someone I would have hoped to remain friends with. I do miss her. In some ways, you remind me of her."

Sharon blanched. "I'm sorry, Ben. I'm not sure

how to take that." Did her likeness to his dead wife explain the long, penetrating looks, the near kiss in the corridor?

"No, I guess I shouldn't have said it. You really don't look like her at all, although she was quite beautiful too. Maybe it's the way you dress, the rushing around after who knows what."

"Excuse me?"

"She travelled a lot for her job. Her choice; she liked it. But sometimes I thought she was running away from me, from our tenuous marriage. She was on her way to a convention on a Fourth of July weekend when the charter plane had crashed. I'd begged her not to go. She'd wanted me to accompany her, but my father left the company in pretty much of a mess, and I was in the midst of unravelling it."

His face tightened with remembered pain.

"I thought then that her staying home would solve our problems. I realize now it would have only accentuated them."

As she listened, Sharon's heart wrenched. Unaware of her actions, she stepped closer and slipped her hand into his. His big hand wrapped automatically around hers, enveloping her in its warmth.

She felt the intensity of the connection as though they were soldered together. His eyes beamed down on hers. Why did she feel so much for a man she'd met only last night? She must be going insane.

"I'm not trying to make a bid for your sympathy," he said. "I didn't mean to tell you all this."

"But you are," she observed, her hand still firmly linked in his. She had no inclination to withdraw it.

"You seem to bring something out in me. Maybe I'm just trying to explain."

"Explain?" she asked, unable to tear her eyes away. They were standing oh so close together in the cold air.

"Something crazy is happening every time we're together. Don't you feel it too?" He knew she did.

Sharon acknowledged it with a slow nod. This chemistry was too strong to deny. She'd be a liar if she did.

"Isn't it perfectly logical?" she asked. "I mean, I'm stranded away from home on a holiday, and you're feeling alone and then, voila, fate throws us together. We each meet someone new, and we're curious." She concluded by shrugging her shoulders.

The problem was, she didn't believe her own explanation. All she kept thinking of was how good it would feel to snuggle into his arms, against his broad chest and taste the kiss he'd nearly bestowed on her a short while ago.

"Maybe," he replied, not believing it either. No one had made him feel like he was skiing through the universe just by their presence, maybe ever. He had too much control to find himself this attracted to her merely on a whim.

"But this is good that we're getting this out in the open," she said. "So we can figure out how to deal with it." The warmth from his hand coursed up her arm, turning it to jelly and setting her nerves tingling. "After all, I'll be gone tomorrow night."

"Back to your boyfriend," he said, carefully gauging her reaction. When her face was not suddenly swathed in bliss, when she did not pull her hand away from his, hope surged in his heart.

"Yes," was all she said, not about to confide she'd already decided she couldn't marry Chris because of her reaction to Ben. It would have sounded absurd. But it wasn't a choice of choosing one over the other. It was a matter of seeing the truth about her feelings for Chris.

"I guess I'm not very successful at long-term relationships," he warned. "So we'd better keep this in check." He added quickly, "Since that's best for both of us."

Reluctantly, he released her slim hand, wishing instead to pull her closer and kiss her leisurely.

Still affected by his warmth, Sharon looked startled. "Of course. I do understand," she agreed.

"What is that perfume you wear?" he asked.

Bewildered, she named it.

Ben nodded, mentally filing the information.

"Did your wife wear it?" she asked.

"No," he answered. "But I assure you it's a scent I will never forget."

Sharon shot him a last glance before moving toward the car. She was beginning to wonder if they shouldn't at least make some attempt to explore this fierce attraction between them. Maybe she didn't want to go home and always question whether she'd miraculously fallen in love with a man on sight.

It was the stuff of fairy tales. She didn't believe in rescued princesses and happily ever after; hadn't since she was a little girl and had waited ever so long for one that never materialized. The only miracles were those you made happen for yourself.

Perhaps if they did chance a kiss, the bubble would burst.

She reminded herself Ben found this attraction as perplexing as she did. And he didn't want to pursue it. She couldn't blame him. If she found herself in a marriage that fell short of her expectations, she wouldn't want to ever fall in love again either.

She sat in the car and decided to comply with Ben's wishes and carefully avoid being alone with him until it was time to go to Atlanta. That should be simple enough.

She glanced at him as he got in the car. He was tall and trim and handsome and so good to her she couldn't stand it. Her mission, she realized, would be as easy to accomplish as trying to avoid the plague.

Chapter Six

They found Sara in the kitchen, crimping the edge of a pie crust.

Her eyes leveled on Sharon's grim expression.

"Doesn't look like good news," she said.

Sharon poured out the story of her car and the flight that wouldn't leave until tomorrow evening.

"I really don't want to put you to any more trouble than I already have," she finished.

Sara brushed her apology off with a wave of one flour-caked hand. "I'm thrilled to have another person here to share the holiday. Take your coat off and don't think another thing about it. You'll just stay here with me as long as necessary."

"I'd better call ... home," she said, unable to resist chancing a glance at Ben behind her. His eyebrows lifted slightly, and she looked away quickly.

"Of course," Sara replied, snatching up a dishtowel to wipe her hands. "You can use the phone upstairs where it's quieter."

"Thank you," Sharon replied, grateful for the older woman's graceful way of safeguarding her privacy. She rushed out of the room without looking at Ben again.

He watched her until she was out of sight, then dropped into one of Sara's kitchen chairs.

"Coffee, Ben?" she asked, already pouring herself a cup.

"Thanks," he said, still looking toward the staircase.

Sara glanced in the same direction. "She's a beautiful girl, isn't she?"

"More than a girl, Aunt Sara," he pointed out. "And yes, she's very pretty. Did you know she's Devan Thomas's granddaughter?"

The color drained from Sara's face. She rarely lost her composure, and the sight was alarming.

"Sara?" Ben said, half rising to help her. "Are you all right?"

"Yes," she insisted with obvious irritation. "I just. . . . Well, it's like you dredged up a ghost."

Ben's eyes focused on her like radar beacons. "I would hate to think it's because our family fortune rests on my grandfather having cheated

Mr. Thomas out of his recipes. Nothing like that happened, did it?"

Sara's slim hand flew to her collar. "Why would you ever say a thing like that? How should I know anything about it? Your grandfather didn't confide in me about his business dealings."

"How did their partnership break up?"

"Ben, leave it be. The past is over and done with and you don't want to start probing into something that's impossible to understand at this point in time."

"I guess I never wondered about it because until now Devan Thomas seemed like more of a vague childhood memory than a real person. I didn't wonder about the recipes until it came up while I was talking to Sharon. If my whole business is based on a lie...." He glanced down at the linoleum.

"I'm sure Mr. Thomas was fairly compensated for his recipes or he would have brought suit against us."

Ben stifled a bitter laugh. "I'm sure Grandfather would have made him believe he couldn't."

Sara's eyes leveled on her nephew. "Is Sharon claiming she has a stake in the company? Is her being here not so much an accident?"

Sharon, in the hallway, stopped dead in her

tracks. She'd been so wrapped up in her frustration at having to talk to Chris's secretary rather than directly to him, that she'd nearly marched into the room without realizing she was being discussed.

"Of course not!" Ben insisted. "But I never have gotten a full explanation of how Grandfather ended up with the company and Mr. Thomas seems to have gotten nothing. Everyone knows he died a pauper."

Sharon shivered involuntarily. Perhaps in the end her grandfather felt he'd been let down somehow too, robbed of those closest to him.

She realized she had to enter the room or momentarily she'd be caught eavesdropping.

As she stepped into the bright, warm kitchen, a stifling silence engulfed the room.

She swung her glance from Ben's tight expression to Sara's.

"I'm afraid I overheard the tail end of your conversation," she admitted. She faced Sara. "And when I came here I knew no more about my grandfather than that he used to live here and once owned a restaurant. I knew nothing of his connection to the fruitcake factory and aside from a genealogical interest, I'm not concerned with pursing the matter of his recipes. As far as I'm concerned, they belong to Ben."

She ended her proclamation with a heavy sigh, feeling as though she'd been on trial.

"I apologize if our conversation made you uncomfortable," Sara said finally. "I suppose I'm overprotective where my family is concerned. And in this case, overly suspicious."

Sharon shrugged. "I don't hold Ben responsible for whatever his grandfather might have done."

Ben knew in that moment he was somehow going to find out one way or the other. He wasn't going to live being absolved of the sins of his grandfather. Either he was going to make certain the recipes were his free and clear or make arrangements to compensate Thomas's heirs.

Sara smiled, a rosy glow returning to her cheeks. "It's best for everybody that way," she proclaimed. She turned to her nephew. "And now, Ben, maybe you could go to work for a while so I can give Sharon the interview I promised. Come back at supper time for chili, and bring Glynis and the boys."

Ben rolled his eyes and flashed a warning glance at Sharon. "She's making a party out of having you here, you realize," he said.

Sharon smiled. The prospect of an evening with the pleasant people she'd met here seemed like a wonderful idea. For the moment, whatever had happened between her grandfather and

Ben's was forgotten. She had no use for the recipes, no desire to disrupt the business of a man who had been nothing but kind to her.

Still, she couldn't dispel the nagging feeling she was letting her grandfather down somehow. Shouldn't she, for the sake of his memory, investigate thoroughly and confirm he wasn't cheated?

She brushed the inclination aside. Too many problems plagued her right now for her to create another.

She looked up at Ben, unprepared for the sudden constricting of her heart as her eyes fell upon his handsome face. "Sounds great," she replied.

Ben shook his head. "I knew the two of you would hit it off together," he murmured as he made his way toward the door.

Drumming his broad hands against the steering wheel, Ben mulled over the morning's events as he drove back to work.

He scanned the familiar twisting streets of his hometown with a surge of affection. As a teenager, he'd often felt oppressed here, eager to make his mark on the big city. But how quickly he'd learned it was the other way around.

The city teemed with anonymous, hopeful faces. Often, it was the city that shaped a person.

Life there grew hard and was sapped of meaning. Here, he could make a difference, maintain a small measure of control in a world that often seemed to have gone mad.

His grandfather would have said he set his sights too low. But Ben had everything he wanted here—almost.

After Yvonne had died, he'd pushed away his dreams of having a family. And when he came home each night, greeted by only his Labrador retriever, he told himself it didn't matter.

The remembered vision of Sharon's delicate features came involuntarily and struck him with something akin to pain. He knew his life was a shallow joke, but one that would have to continue. Maybe he just wasn't capable of sharing enough to make a relationship work. Maybe that's the legacy he'd inherited from his grandfather.

Timothy Russell was a stingy, mean-spirited man. But Ben had loved him. As a boy he'd looked up to the man who always took a keen interest in him. It was only as he grew older that he steadily began to realize Timothy's generosity did not extend beyond his family and that his love for Ben was a selfish thing.

Perhaps the realization that Timothy was grooming Ben as his heir was the thing that had sent him fleeing to the city. As if distance could break the genetic tie that could make him become the kind of man his grandfather was.

Ben laughed softly to himself. How ironic it was that he ran his grandfather's business today. Ben liked to think his motives were different. Of course he made a good living, but he also provided many jobs in the community. That meant more to him than it ever had to his grandfather.

Had Timothy cheated Sharon's grandfather? Ben swore he'd find out.

The consequences could be bleak. What if Sharon and her family still had a legal claim on the company? An outsider wouldn't care about jobs and this town.

Maybe it would be better to leave it be as Sara had advised him.

But in good conscience he couldn't. He'd start digging through the records this afternoon.

He parked in front of the plant and walked into the front office.

"You look as though your mind's a million miles away," Glynis offered.

Ben broke out of his reverie. "Just thinking," he offered. "I'm going to be out in the back where the old files are for a while. By the way, Sara's invited you and the boys for chili tonight."

Glynis's expression grew solem. "Before you escape, I guess I'd better tell you what's going on. I called Sara's, but she said you were already on your way back here. Tom had to leave. His wife's in labor, and he's taken her to the hospital."

Ben snapped back to the reality of having a business to run in its peak season of the year with customers and employees depending on him.

His eyes widened. "I thought the baby wasn't due for a couple of weeks."

Glynis shrugged. "It's not. He was just frantic. Evelyn's covering for him."

Ben nodded. He went to a small closet and extracted a white apron, then headed for the hallway toward the bakery area. Tom was his best floor supervisor, and his absence left a huge gap. Ben himself would cover for him this afternoon.

"Send some flowers to the hospital," he instructed Glynis on the way out. Everything else would just have to wait.

Sharon's tension dissipated as she sat beside Sara Eagleston's fireplace and sipped a mug of cocoa. For the first time in a long while, she felt warm and rested and calm.

Maybe it was because of her decision about Chris, she considered. Hadn't she always, without realizing it, felt pressured? He would be disappointed, she knew, if she didn't apply for and get Millicent's job when she left. But she had postponed turning in her application because she didn't want the position.

Or maybe her sense of well-being stemmed from the soft crackling of the fire, or the growing friendship between her and Sara. If Sara mistrusted her, she'd given no sign of it this afternoon. The interview had gone well. The museum patrons would have a new glimpse of this artist's life and work.

But when she looked up and saw Ben enter the room with a magnificent golden dog at his heels, her pulse got thready, and she knew he was responsible.

She could love him if it were possible.

But she pushed the idea aside. There was no chance of it.

The dog eagerly ran to her, jumping up and nearly upsetting the mug of cocoa in her hand.

"Star!" he reprimanded sternly.

The dog reluctantly removed her paws, sitting before Sharon and staring at her with wide brown eyes.

"She's trying to say hello," Ben told her. "She wants you to pet her."

Sharon's eyes shifted warily from the dog to Ben, then back again.

"She won't bite?" she asked.

"She won't bite you," he said, appraising the woman in the easy chair. Sharon looked different tonight, but he couldn't pinpoint what had changed. Her skin was flushed from the heat of the fire, but it was more than that. She looked relaxed—almost as if she belonged here.

She continued staring at Star.

"Haven't you ever had a dog?" he asked.

She shook her head. "No dogs, no cats. My uncle's allergic."

Ben stepped closer, then knelt down beside his dog. Sharon's skin tingled. She was as aware of his closeness as she was of the heat of the fire.

Star licked Ben's face generously. Dodging the slurpy kisses, he pushed her back slightly with his big hands and rustled the fur on her head.

"She might overwhelm you with affection, but she won't hurt you," he told Sharon.

Sharon reached out and patted the dog's head as Ben restrained his pet from jumping into her lap. Star nuzzled her wrist.

"She's a beautiful animal," Sharon offered as her hand glided down the back of Star's neck, along the smooth fur.

"I've had her since she was a pup," Ben said.

His eyes turned upward to meet hers, and he caught the light powdery scent of her perfume. Whatever the change in her, she looked exceptionally beautiful tonight. Maybe he only noticed more tonight because he knew tomorrow she'd be out of his life forever.

Was he going to let her go? What choice did he have? Of course she would go. He wouldn't see her again.

Impulsively, his glance unwavering, he caught her fingertips in his.

Her eyes flared slightly and continued to meet his as the warmth of his hand coursed up her arm, paralyzing her with its intensity.

He thought how his position resembled that of a man proposing marriage, then he thought how bright and clear her eyes were and how he would like to know what was going on behind them.

Sharon thought how much she liked the touch of him, the firm grip of his hand on hers, and how much she would like to hold on and follow wherever he might lead.

A silly impulse. More daring than anything she'd ever attempted.

With him so close, it was difficult to think clearly. No one had ever scrambled her senses with his mere presence—only Ben.

Dimly, she heard the voice of her aunt telling her, "Lose your heart, but never lose your head. You'll live with the consequences a long time."

Sharon wondered whether that advice stemmed from her older cousin eloping with a man her aunt and uncle didn't approve of, or if it had something to do with the silent lack of affection in their own functional but lackluster marriage.

And she wondered if her heart would ever start beating normally again, and if it would ever stop aching after she left this place. She'd found something here she'd never really believed in since she was a little girl.

Ben raised his free hand to her glistening hair, capturing a strand of it between his fingers.

"Sharon," he said, his voice low as if he were telling her a secret. Her own name had never never sounded so musical or magical before.

Without realizing it, she leaned down closer to him, as if compelled by a hypnotic suggestion, forgetting her qualms about the dog beside him.

Suddenly, Sara's voice broke through the silence as she strolled into the room. "I was wondering when you'd get here, Ben."

Sharon's head jerked upward at the sound, her face burning.

"I got tied up at work," Ben said distractedly, his attention still focused on Sharon.

Sara stood in the archway with her hands on her hips, surprise spreading over her face as she took in the scene before her.

She smiled down on them as though she'd just unwrapped a birthday gift.

"Excuse me," she said slyly, turning back toward the kitchen. Her voice trailed down the hallway. "I've forgotten to grate the cheese." She stopped midway and called back, "If he's proposing, honey, say yes."

Sharon's eyes rounded. Her face reddened as bright as a ripe apple in autumn.

Ben wondered briefly if it would be such a terrible idea—throwing caution to blazes and holding Sharon close to him for the rest of their lives. Then he remembered what happened the last time he'd believed love could conquer the vast, real differences between the way two people chose to live.

He slowly released Sharon's hand, then reached up and relieved her of the mug she'd held suspended in midair and set it on the coffee table.

"Lousy timing," he noted.

"Or good timing," Sharon suggested, able to pull her wits together now that the spell was broken.

"Was it?" he asked, getting to his feet.

Sharon gazed up at him. He seemed a giant hovering over her.

What did he want, a confession of her feelings? She didn't know what they were herself. And to what end?

He stood over her waiting for an answer. He'd known just moments ago she was feeling something for him, something possibly as strong as the overwhelming tenderness he felt toward her.

But if she couldn't acknowledge that, there was nowhere to go.

Ben waited for an answer.

Sharon searched for words. She realized she was good at planning and analyzing but lost when it came to putting her real feelings into words. For so many years, she'd always done what was expected of her and kept her emotions to herself. It was instinct, a survival instinct. In a pinch, she always retreated to that secret place inside herself. It was a place that until now, no one had ever tried to invade.

She'd spent the early part of her life trying to please, not to communicate, she discovered.

Ben put his hands to his hips and looked down on Sharon. What was she hiding behind all that loveliness? he wondered. He suspected he'd never know.

After one last hard look, he turned and walked toward the kitchen, calling Star behind him.

Sharon watched him walk away, filled with the deepest sense of abandonment she'd ever experienced.

"Ben," she called after him softly, but he

either didn't hear or didn't acknowledge and kept walking.

Blinking back unexplained tears, Sharon reached for the mug, swilling her cocoa before she realized it was as cold as mud.

Chapter Seven

Sharon barely tasted the scorching chili. As she stabbed her spoon into her bowl, she was aware of Ben's broad shoulder inches from hers—the outdoorsy scent of him, the heat of his skin beneath his shirt sleeve. Sara, misinterpreting what she'd witnessed in the living room, had seated them side-by-side at the long dinner table.

But Sharon sensed Ben had closed himself off to her now. She felt wounded and reminded herself she had no right to.

Across the table, Glynis was keeping up a lively conversation, flanked on both sides by her strapping teenage sons. The older one had brought his girlfriend, a slender girl with straight blonde hair, who from time to time flashed adoring blue eyes on her.

Sharon thought of her own teenage years. Joe

Hamilton had faded into a dim memory now, but she'd had the biggest crush on him for a long time. She'd thought all her dreams were coming true when he'd asked her out.

But her aunt had taken the light out of her eyes by reminding her she needed to concentrate on building a solid future. She needed a career in which she could support herself.

The unspoken message was always clear, Sharon reflected. Once she graduated, there would be no place for her in her aunt's house.

So, she'd broken off with a bewildered Joe and run home to cry herself to sleep.

Looking back, she wondered why she hadn't been more defiant. But she knew she'd always been afraid of losing even more, of having to live with other strangers.

She realized she had nothing to fear now. She was responsible for guiding her life. So why did she feel so afraid?

She wasn't so sure anymore she knew where she wanted to take it. She realized she had nearly plunged unaware into a marriage that would have been as tedious as her aunt and uncle's.

"So Tom's a father," Glynis reported, beaming over her chili. "How's Anna doing?"

"I only stopped by for a minute," Ben replied.

"I don't think I've ever seen Tom so keyed up, but he said everyone is doing fine."

Sharon stared down at her food as though the conversation were taking place somewhere far away.

"Your chili's getting cold."

She looked up to see Ben glancing down at her over his shoulder. She studied his pleasant features and suddenly she longed to tell him everything about her and hope he'd understand.

Why did it matter so much to her what he above everyone else thought?

"I guess I've lost my appetite," she said.

"I hope you're not coming down with something," Sara said from the head of the table. "I'd never forgive myself."

"I'm sure I'll be fine," Sharon insisted, unwilling to cause her hostess any further concern. "I just shouldn't have had that cocoa before dinner."

Sara eyed her intently. "You do look a little pale. Can I get you something instead of this spicy chili? I've got some leftover soup in the refrigerator."

Sharon shook her head. "No, please. This is fine."

Sara turned to Ben. "Why don't you take Sharon outside for some air? That fire and all the cooking have made it stuffy in here."

Sharon got to her feet. Putting some distance between herself and Ben might alleviate her distress. "Some fresh air does seem like a good idea. But I can go on my own."

"Ben has to take his dog out," Sara said, casting a look at Star, who was innocently sprawled across her rag rug.

Ben rose, pushing the chair in and whistling for the dog, who immediately sprang to life. "Some air might not be a bad idea," he agreed, guiding Sharon toward the front door.

His hand resting lightly on her waist triggered a keen awareness inside her. Her pulse quickened, and her skin grew hot.

He retrieved their coats from the closet. "It's cold outside," he offered, wrapping hers around her shoulders. Then he opened the door, and she stepped under the arch of his arm, avoiding his eyes.

The frigid air washed over them.

"In case you didn't catch on, my aunt is trying to get us alone together," he said after he closed the door and caught up to walk alongside her. Star ran on ahead into the woods.

"I suppose she's gotten the wrong idea," Sharon said.

"Are you all right?"

"I'm fine, really. I just wasn't very hungry."

They followed the path Star had taken. Even

in the darkness, she felt his eyes scorching her. She stopped midstride.

Ben followed suit, turning toward her. Cloaked by his shadow in the iridescent moonlight, she involuntarily took a step backward only to feel the hard trunk of a tree against her back.

Ben stared down at her, remembering the giddy feeling of being a boy and finding an exceptionally pretty butterfly, watching it flutter across the fields as the patterns on its flapping wings displayed a kaleidoscope of color.

This is what he'd found here, something rare and fragile and beautiful. Should he capture it or let it fly away?

Ignoring common sense, he let the surge of awakening flow through him.

"Have you considered maybe it's not so wrong?" he asked. "Maybe life isn't meant to be quite so logical and sane as we'd like it to be?"

Sharon's breath caught in her chest. He was standing so close, casting a magnificent silhouette. She could think of little else but his overwhelming presence.

When she breathed, a puff of steam drifted into the air.

"This is absurd," she insisted, barely getting the words out because just then his lips covered hers. His mouth fell on her softly and eagerly.

He tasted sweet and mellow like chocolate covered marshmallows, and she could think of nothing but the sensation of being wrapped in honeycomb.

Her hands rested on his shoulders as his arms folded around her. In his embrace she felt tiny, and as the kiss ended and he cradled her head against the bulk of his chest, a peacefulness rippled through her like the lazy current of a river.

This had been destined to happen from the moment they collided, she realized. She didn't want it to end, although she knew it had to.

A jingling sound startled her, and she tensed in his arms.

"It's only Star coming back," he whispered, pressing her head back down against his chest. But reality had intruded.

"We'd better get back," she suggested, reluctantly pulling away from him.

But he didn't release her immediately, gazing down on her in a way that made her heart pound.

Finally, he asked, "That guy back home. Are you going to marry him?"

Sharon looked up at him. "Obviously, I lack sufficient commitment to do that," she replied. Did he think, she wondered, that she would have returned his kiss if she intended to go home and marry Chris?

"Maybe I was out of line just now. But I'm not

sorry it happened. And deep down, I don't think you are either."

Sharon looked up at him, her lips turning upward into a soft smile that pulled at his heart. She raised one hand to his face, grazing his rough cheek with the back of her hand.

"I have trouble sometimes sorting out my feelings," she confessed. "I guess I kept them under wraps so long I stopped knowing what they are. But you've helped me see the truth about my relationship with Chris and probably saved me from an unhappy marriage. And for that, I thank you."

Was that it? Ben wondered, his eyes narrowing, spine stiffening. Thank you?

Wasn't it though? He could ask to see her again. But to what end? The holidays would be over before he could get away from work long enough to even go see her. And by then she would have convinced herself a passing attraction wasn't worth sacrificing an established relationship for. He would have remembered he was making the same mistake he'd made with Yvonne. They'd both borne the consequences of that!

Maybe "thank you" would just have to be enough. He had no promises to offer. Yet she didn't seem to expect any. And maybe that's what made him want to give them all the more.

"You'll go back to him," Ben predicted.

"I don't think so," Sharon returned, hoping he wasn't right. She too knew things would appear different once she was home, far away from Ben. She would plan her future in the logical manner she always did.

But what she felt for Ben came straight from the heart, untainted by cold sanity.

Nothing had ever felt so wonderful and delicious. She hadn't dreamed anything ever could.

She realized she didn't want to leave at all. But he wasn't asking anything of her, wasn't speculating or promising. She surmised he'd closed himself off after his wife died.

Avoiding his eyes, she shrugged. "I suppose we both just need somebody right now. That's why this happened. We both know this is all that will come of it."

His voice was husky in the cold night. "That's not what I want."

Sharon raked her hair back with splayed fingers. "What do you want?"

"I don't know," he answered helplessly.

Sharon laughed lightly, her mouth bursting into a gorgeous smile. "In that respect, we're a prefect pair."

He smiled down on her, his heavy hand caressing the soft hollow of her throat. Fever rushed through her, despite the wintry air. Her chin tilted upward.

"We've one thing in common. That's a start," he said, leaning down and gracing her with a leisurely powerful kiss that robbed her of all her senses. In that moment she knew whatever existed between them was something she'd never find with anyone else.

His breath fell warmly across her cheek as he pulled back mere inches and spoke. "Let's not go in just yet."

"All right," she said, sensing everything would change under the bright light of Sara's porcelain lamps.

He wrapped one arm around her, and she leaned against him as they strolled down the darkened path into the woods. To a backdrop of Star's tags jingling through the trees like distant sleighbells, she began to tell him the things she'd sheltered in her heart for many years.

In a place she'd never been before with a man she barely knew, she felt at last safe and free.

Ben listened patiently, eagerly, masking his surprise. The more he heard, the less she reminded him of Yvonne. Sharon, he discovered, was a sweet and gentle person hiding behind the exterior of a tough, independent businesswoman because that's what she'd believed she had to do to survive.

And he ached to free the scared wounded woman inside her, but he didn't know if he could. Or dared.

When they reached the house, Glynis's red Toyota was no longer in the drive.

"Glynis must have gone home," Ben observed.

"I hope she won't think we were rude."

"I don't care what she thinks," he said, gazing down on her. "I enjoyed the evening."

"I talked too much."

He shook his head. "There's no shame in saying what you think."

"I don't think anyone's ever listened the way you have."

"If you ever need someone to listen, just call."

"Right," Sharon said, remembering suddenly the impossible distance between them. She wouldn't be calling him. It would be too painful, to hear him and not be able to see him or touch him.

Ben felt a deep stirring inside him. He hadn't felt this close to anyone in a long time, maybe ever. Yet he couldn't volunteer more than some limp offer for her to call. She wouldn't.

"We'd better go inside," he said, resisting the urge to kiss her a third time. If he did, it would all pour out—the emotions, the promises. He'd invade her life with expectations he knew he couldn't live up to.

With bittersweet reluctance, he opened the front door. A pool of light splashed out.

Sharon stepped inside and he followed, summoning Star.

"I'm in here," Sara called.

Tracing her voice to the kitchen, they found her wrestling with a frozen turkey.

Ben stepped forward and relieved her of the bird. "Where do you want it?" he asked.

She pointed to the countertop. He set it down atop a dishtowel.

"Are you sure this thing is going to thaw by morning?" he asked.

"No," Sara answered. "But it has to. I made some coffee. Do you two want some?"

"Something hot to drink sounds good," Ben said, unwilling to leave just yet.

Sara, apparently psychic, already had three mugs set out on the counter. "It's getting colder outside, isn't it?" she asked as they slid into chairs at the table and slipped their coats off.

"Yes, it is," Sharon said. She smiled back at Ben as he grinned at her across the table. *If only he knew, her heart was in his hands,* she thought.

Setting the mugs on the table, Sara caught the looks passing between the two of them. Saying nothing, she got her own mug and dropped into a vacant chair between them.

"The weather report says there might be snow tonight," she informed them.

"Snow?" Sharon asked incredulously.

Ben's eyes danced. "Not much of that in Florida, is there?"

"Not any I've ever seen," Sharon admitted.

"Don't worry," he assured her. "I've got tire chains, so unless the airport closes, you'll still be able to get home."

Sharon's smile fell. Right now, she felt as though she wouldn't mind if ten feet of snow forced her to stay here until spring. But of course she'd forgotten she was imposing on Sara and Ben as well. She forced her smile back in place.

Sara waved one hand in the air, clutching her mug with the other. "Snow is predicted here far more often than it actually falls. It would be pretty for the holiday and all though."

"I wouldn't mind seeing some," Sharon admitted.

"We'll see what nature can whip up for you," Ben offered.

Sara leaned over the table, propping her chin on one arm. "I just love Thanksgiving. I think it's one of my favorite holidays."

"Why?" Sharon asked.

"Because I've got so much to be thankful for,

of course. If you ask me, once a year's not nearly often enough to dwell on how lucky we are."

Sharon took a mental inventory. Finding Ben loomed first on her list. Funny, she thought, how her whole life had so suddenly and drastically shifted out of focus? Or was it in focus now?

Sara turned sharply as the phone rang. She began getting up to answer it, but oddly, it didn't ring again.

"I guess someone realized they had the wrong number," she said, easing back into her chair.

Ben rose and put his jacket on, leaving his coffee untouched on the tabletop. "I guess I'd better go. I have to go into the plant early to clear up some paperwork."

"On Thanksgiving?" Sara asked with horror. "You work entirely too hard."

"So do you, Sara," he countered.

"But I do it because I'm old and have nothing else to do," she quipped. Her eyes leveled on him. "You'll be surprised to see one day how fast the days slip away and the good times are gone. You're far too serious. Have some fun while you're still young."

"Good night, Sara," he said, casting an indulgent look before he leaned over and grazed her cheek with his lips.

He moved toward Sharon, and she feared for

a moment he would lean over and kiss her as well, but instead, he grabbed her by the hand.

"Walk me to the door?" he asked.

Wordlessly, she got up and walked with him. She avoided looking back at Sara, but she knew the woman was smiling.

As they reached the foyer, Ben stopped in the doorway, turning to her. Silently, he studied her face, probing the silver of her eyes. Sharon felt a churning in her chest.

He caught her other hand in his free one. Glancing over his shoulder to be sure Sara hadn't followed, he said, "I dread tomorrow, knowing you're leaving."

"I guess that's as inevitable as our collision was," Sharon said, her eyes sweeping over the planes of his face, struggling to imprint it in her memory.

He nodded solemnly. "We won't mention it tomorrow, then. We'll just enjoy the day, being together, and when it's time, I'll take you to the airport."

"All right," she agreed. It wouldn't make her leaving go away. But if it was what he wanted, she'd go along with it.

He smiled down on her. "If I didn't know better, I'd say I was falling in love with you."

His words tore through her like spears.

How did he know "better"? She'd already realized if this wasn't love, she didn't know what it was and would never know.

The shadow of his dead wife had fallen over them, she realized. He'd said they weren't happy, but he must have believed at first he loved her. She didn't know if Ben would ever be free of that ghost.

Perhaps her leaving was the best thing after all.

"I'll see you tomorrow," she said, resisting the urge to lean forward and press her lips to his.

"Tomorrow," he said. Releasing her gently, he called his dog.

When he opened the door the cold air blew in like a sobering shower. She watched out the window as he opened the car door. Star leapt inside, then he got in, closed the door, and started the engine.

"Mercy," she said under her breath.

"What?"

She jumped, startled to find Sara had walked up behind her.

"Nothing," she said quickly. "I was just thinking out loud."

"Hmm," Sara said. "I take it my nephew wasn't proposing earlier then."

"Ben's not looking for another wife," Sharon said.

Sara laughed lightly. "He just doesn't know he is. I noticed the way he looks at you."

"I don't think he and I are right for each other, although I do like him."

Sara's brow furrowed. "Were you using the phone on the desk in the den earlier?"

"No," Sharon replied, thinking the question odd. There were phones in the bedroom and the kitchen. She wouldn't even enter the den without asking permission, much less use the phone in there.

"It was off the hook," Sara mused, folding her arms across her chest. "I suppose Glynis or one of the kids might have slipped in there to make a call and not set it back completely on the cradle."

Sharon smiled at the woman. "Can I help you with the dinner preparations? You've been so good to me. There must be something I can do."

Sara shook her head. "Not tonight. I'm ready to turn in. But there'll be plenty you can help me with in the morning."

"Okay. I've never prepared a Thanksgiving dinner before, and I'm only now realizing what a lot of work it is."

"The work's half the fun. It takes a long time, where eating all the food only requires about fifteen minutes and it's over."

"The work is the fun?"

"The anticipation, you know. If you don't enjoy preparing for things, your life just slips right by you. I mean, that's ninety percent of life, isn't it? How much of our lives we spend getting ready for things we don't even know are coming. My art, for example. I lived a lot of years unaware I could hold a paintbrush. But when I stand over a canvas, I'm calling up resources I've aquired through my whole life."

"Don't you ever wish you'd started earlier?" Sharon asked.

Sara shook her head. "Good things in good time. The sin comes in when you're ready for something and turn your back on it."

Sharon swallowed hard. Like falling in love and walking away? Was that a sin? No, she told herself. She couldn't stay with someone who wanted her to leave.

"I am tired," Sharon said. "I'll see you in the morning, Sara."

"Good night, dear. I can't tell you how much I'm enjoying having you here."

Touched, Sharon turned. "Thank you. I feel as though I'm visiting a relative I never knew I had."

"Maybe you'll come back," the older woman suggested.

"Maybe," Sharon agreed.

But she knew she wouldn't. She had too much

pride to come back, knowing Ben was here, unless he himself asked. And he wasn't going to.

"Good night, Sara," she said.

"Good night, dear. Pleasant dreams."

Chapter Eight

Despite the warm, comfortable bed she was nestled in, Sharon slept restlessly, plagued not by dreams but by dim distressing thoughts.

In the late hours of the night, she finally tumbled into a deeper sleep, and by the time she woke, daylight was streaming in through the windows.

Opening her eyes, she propped herself up on her elbows, taking a minute to recall where she was and what was going on. As she remembered this would be her last day here with Ben, her spirits fell.

But she recalled Sara's words last night. She would not, she promised herself, mope about their inevitable parting. She would enjoy the day, as she'd agreed to with Ben last night.

Fully awake now, she looked toward the window, her eyes flaring as she took in the blanket of white that had fallen in the night.

"Snow!" she exclaimed joyfully, smiling at the wonder of it. She'd never seen anything more precious and delicate and lovely.

Shooting out of bed, she ran barefoot to the window like an awe-struck child.

It's incredible, she thought as she leaned on the sill and took in the wooded landscape. Unmarred by footprints or soot, it draped the treetops and bushes and rolling hills. She only wished she could have seen it falling. That sight would have been worth sitting up all night for.

And by some magic, this miracle of nature gave her hope. Surely, everything would be right today.

Like a vision, Ben's car came scooting slowly up the driveway, leaving a set of tracks in the fresh-fallen snow. A grin brightened Sharon's face as she watched the door open. Down below, Star bounded out, dancing around and leaving a splattering of tiny pawprints in the powdery snow.

Ben stepped out next. Sharon didn't realize he could see her until he looked up and waved. She waved back, unmindful of her night clothes or her uncombed hair until he proceeded toward the front door.

Panic siezed her, and her hand flew up to her

head. She had to get dressed immediately or the snow might melt before she got out in it. And Ben was here. Every moment she could spend with him was precious.

With reckless speed, she threw on jeans and a sweater, washed her face and combed her hair, not bothering with makeup. Rushing down-stairs, she found Ben and Sara in the kitchen having coffee.

The house already teemed with the smell of roasting turkey, and she felt guilty for having stayed in bed so long. She'd promised Sara she'd help prepare this afternoon's meal.

Her eyes flew to the clock, and she was sur-prised to see it was only just past nine.

"Good morning." Ben greeted her with a long, slow stare that set her heart racing.

"Good morning," she replied, feeling the warmth she'd come to associate with him course through her. She turned to Sara. "I should have been up earlier to help you with the turkey."

"No problem," Sara said good naturedly. "I like getting up early, while the world is still quiet. Thought I might as well go ahead and put the turkey on. Nothing's as frustrating as one that doesn't ever seem to want to get done."

"What she means," Ben added. "Is that she wants to do things by herself so she can do them her own way."

Sara dismissed him with a wave of her hand. "So," she said. "What do you think of your snow-fall?"

"It's wonderful," Sharon replied.

Sara nodded. "You'd better go out and play in it before the sun comes out and melts it."

Ben smiled at her. "I've brought an extra pair of gloves." He dangled them in the air.

"Are you coming out too?" she asked Sara.

Sara shook her head. "I've seen it before, and I'd rather just look at it through the window. You two go on, and I'll have breakfast ready when you get back."

Sharon hesitated.

Ben stood. "Come on. You wished for this. Now you've got to have the total snow experience, so you'll have something to talk about when you get home."

Her nerves twitched with the reminder she was leaving today. But she masked the heavy sadness that was building inside her.

"Sure," she said, going for her coat.

Ben waited for her at the front door.

"Hold out your hands," he instructed.

When she obeyed, he pulled a thick glove over each. "Wouldn't want your skin to get chapped," he suggested.

She felt the heat of him as he leaned over her, and willed herself to ignore it.

His eyes hung on hers for a long moment. He felt as though he were drowning. Even without benefit of makeup, her face was fine and compelling, the pink of her lips as faint as the color of rose petals.

He told himself to stop thinking of her this way. They were strangers who had met unexpectedly and who would part later that evening. And each of their lives would return to what they had been before the accident.

It had to be that way, he assured himself.

He opened the door. "The winter wonders await," he announced.

Star, disgruntled at having been left outside with her wet paws, bounced around her eagerly. Sharon reached out and patted the dog's head.

"Now what?" she asked, her eyes sweeping over the pristine countryside.

"I have a surprise," he told her, walking toward his car with keys in hand. He unlocked the trunk and produced a sled.

"You're kidding," she commented.

"You're not scared to ride it, are you?"

"Of course not. Is the snow deep enough?"

"I guess we'll find out." He pointed to a hill in the distance. "There's the best place to try it out. Come on."

Walking alongside him, she liked the way the

air smelled and how the cold seemed less bothersome when there was snow on the ground.

"I've never seen anything so magnificent," she confessed, as they left two sets of tracks in the new snow.

"It plays tricks on you," Ben warned. "Makes the world look brighter than it is."

At the moment, Sharon didn't care. "Maybe that's something I've needed," she admitted.

Ben reached out and caught her gloved hand in his.

Sharon held on tight, liking the feeling of completeness she experienced.

They walked on in a quiet, satisfied silence, as if there were no one and nothing else in this bleached, still world.

Climbing the hill was treacherous, especially in Sharon's smooth-soled shoes. But whenever she felt herself slipping, Ben's strong arms were always there for her.

Finally, they reached the top. Sharon looked down majestically upon the rest of the world and drew in a deep breath. "Do you do this every time it snows?"

He shook his head. "I haven't been sledding in a long time. I just kept the sled around for my nephews when they'd visit." He studied her. "You kind of lose track, you know, of things that used to be fun."

"I'm glad you thought of it today."

He gestured expansively. "You go down first."

"Me?" She eyed the sled apprehensively.

Ben demonstrated how to get on the sled, how to steer it.

"Piece of cake," she said with false bravado as she rolled her eyes and mounted the sled.

"I'll push you off," he volunteered. "Hold on."

"Okay," she agreed, face-down, staring at the steep slope and wondering if she'd gone insane to have agreed to this.

She felt his slight push, then felt herself careening down the hill, the cold air whipping at her face. The frozen landscape rushed by. The thrill of it overrode the terror.

And it was over in seconds. The sled slowed as it reached level ground. Sharon wondered how to stop it.

Star pranced alongside the careening sled, and as it came to a stop, jumped right on top of her.

"Hey!" Sharon called out, struggling to remove the animal, who was making a fierce attempt to lick her face.

Ben was there in seconds, and she wondered how he'd gotten down the hill so fast.

"Star!" he commanded, and at the sound of his stern voice, the dog immediately jumped off. He reached down and helped Sharon to her feet, expecting to find her angry and upset. Instead, he discovered she was laughing, her face red and rosy from the cold.

"Your dog," she informed him when she finally caught her breath, "is absolutely nuts."

"She likes you," Ben explained with a shrug, relieved she was all right.

Sharon's countenance grew serious. Her eyes levelled on Ben's. "And her master?"

Ben looked down on Sharon's sweet face, thinking how unfair it was that she was so beautiful. A warm tenderness rippled through him, an emotion more powerful than any he'd felt in a long time.

He reached out and swept back a handful of her silky hair. "Her master cares about you enough to want you to be happy."

And Sharon knew true happiness would come to her only if she could be with him. But she couldn't say that, couldn't push him that way. She knew from experience the folly of staying where she wasn't wanted.

Ben wanted to take her in his arms and hold her close. But he reminded himself he didn't have the right.

"I'm starting to think about breakfast now, how about you?" he said finally.

Sharon shook her head. "You haven't had your sleigh ride yet."

"Well, I've done it before."

"I'll believe it when I see it. Fair's fair. If I can ride this thing, so can you. I'll wait down here for you."

Ben gave her a long look. "You're a hard woman, Sharon Hunicutt."

"I just want to be sure you wouldn't have me do anything you wouldn't do yourself."

She watched as Ben towed the sled back up the hill, waving down to her before he mounted the sled and rode it down.

"Happy now?" he asked.

Happier than I've been in a long time, Sharon reflected. Looking back, she didn't think she'd played much as a child. It wasn't that she hadn't been allowed to; it was her own doing. Her mind had always been on more grown-up worries.

How easy and free she felt out here with Ben. She couldn't imagine Chris riding the child's size sled down a hill. He was too much like her, she realized.

And maybe out here, she could be herself, act like a child if she wanted to because she didn't have to measure up to standards anyone else had set for her. Even to the standards she had set for herself.

And Ben's accepting her for herself was a treasure she didn't want to let go of.

"Yes, I am," she answered, wondering what

he would think if he knew the depth behind those words.

"Good," he snapped back. "Can we go eat now?"

Sharon laughed, and Ben savored the way her face lit up.

"I'm hungry too," she admitted, acknowledging the gnawing in her stomach. "Besides, I feel guilty leaving Sara alone so long."

"You shouldn't. Sara's happiest when she thinks things are going her way."

Sharon was about to ask him what he meant by that when something fluttered in front of her face. Her eyes widened with delight.

"A snowflake!" she said with a gasp.

Ben looked up at the gray sky. The sunlight that cut through the clouds earlier had faded. "You must have some powerful influence over the heavens. This is more snow than we've had in years. I think you've forgotten something."

"What's that?" she asked as she reached out to catch a spiraling flake.

"Planes don't fly if there's too much snow."

Her smile dropped. "I had forgotten," she admitted softly. If she had to stay longer, Ben might not be able to get away to take her to the airport. And the prospect of leaving grew more difficult with every moment she stayed.

Ben caught her worried expression and assumed it meant she was anxious to get home. After all, she was stranded here.

He realized he'd broken his own rule. Hoisting the sled and tucking it under one arm, he said, "We can worry about that when the time comes."

But even the flurry of snowflakes couldn't dispel the gloom that had fallen over her. She'd never been a person to run away from problems, and that's what she was doing here, hiding really.

She had to go home and face the reality of what she was, a person who enjoyed her job as assistant director at the museum, working with people. She didn't want to be director and spend more time with paperwork, less time with people.

And she had to face the truth about her and Chris as well. He had a right to know as soon as possible how she felt.

Then somehow she'd piece her life back together and maybe head in the right direction this time.

"Sure," she agreed. "It's bound to stop in a while."

She remained silent the rest of the way to Sara's house.

As soon as she opened the front door the smell of turkey and other delicious aromas mingled in the air, making her stomach churn all the more.

In the warmth of the house, she realized how thoroughly chilled she'd been. Shedding her wet coat, gloves, and shoes, she put them in the laundry room to dry. Ben followed suit.

By the time she returned to the kitchen, Sara had set out a feast of scrambled eggs, bacon, biscuits and cantaloupe wedges.

Ravenous, Sharon sampled all of it. The eggs tasted of herbs and cheddar cheese.

"I wonder how we'll have an appetite left for turkey later?" she asked as she spread strawberry jam across half a biscuit.

"Maybe we'll have to go sledding again," Ben suggested, his eyes twinkling. To her chagrin, he winked at her.

Sharon quickly looked back down at her food. Why did she have to like him so much? He was totally impossible.

Sara drained the last sip of coffee from her mug. "If you two wouldn't mind cleaning up, I think I'm going to go into my studio and paint for a while."

"Isn't there anything else you want me to do?" Sharon asked. "For later?"

Sara looked thoughtful. "I believe everything is ready. You and Ben could start a fire if you want. It would be awfully cozy with the snow outside."

As she left the room, Sharon turned to Ben.

She wondered why she suddenly felt uncomfortable being alone with him.

"I'll take the dishes if you'll take the fire," she suggested.

"Done," he agreed.

Sharon was glad to have a task to occupy her hands if not her mind. Soon she had the dishwasher humming and the countertops sparkling and smelling faintly of pine.

Drying her hands, she peeked into the oven at the small turkey browning and popping. She remembered smelling her aunt's turkeys cooking on holidays and thinking how she would cook her own someday for a family that truly belonged to her.

She'd pushed that dream so far back in her mind, she'd nearly forgotten it until now. Chris had said he might want children someday, an idea so vague it struck her now he never really would. And he'd convinced her she didn't want any either because they would stand in the way of her career and the posh house they were going to have. She'd believed he meant they should wait to have a family. Now, she acknowledged the truth.

Holding on to a future with her and Chris rambling around a lavish house had been a poor substitute for what she really wanted, she thought. She envisioned a big man barreling down a snowy hill on tiny sled and imagined his nephews must enjoy their Uncle Ben enormously.

Carefully shutting the oven door, feeling as though she'd been spying, she walked to the living room and found Ben in a rocker, staring into the fire with the lights off.

"It is nice, isn't it?" she asked, sitting down Indian style on the floor in front of the fireplace.

"Hypnotic," he agreed. "Isn't it odd how the simplest things can be the most enjoyable? Snow. Food. Fire."

"And how rarely we take the time to look at them," she noted, almost as if she were talking to the flames rather than to him. The fire was warm, soothing.

Suddenly, she turned her head to look up at him. "I don't regret having been stranded here," she said.

Ben looked down at the porcelain face highlighted by flickering firelight. His heart flooded with affection for her.

"I'm glad," he said. "I couldn't think of a better place for you to have been stranded." This was too close to saying good-bye, he knew. And he didn't want to think about that right now.

Sharon knew she was treading in dangerous territory. She was coming too close to telling Ben how she really felt about him. And she was uncertain what his reaction would be. She didn't want him to feel obligated to say things he didn't mean.

She looked out the window. The snow was falling fierce and hard, shutting out the rest of the world.

It's like a dream, she thought. *And when I wake up, it will all be over.*

"Sharon."

She awakened to the sound of her own name, a firm hand on her shoulder, a slight shaking.

"What?" she murmured.

"Wake up. It's nearly time for dinner."

She opened her eyes, staring into Ben's as he hovered over her.

"Oh my gosh," she said, as she realized she'd fallen asleep on the carpet. "How long have I been sleeping?"

"Just a few hours."

"How rude," she said, raking fingers through her hair. "I left you sitting there by yourself."

"It's okay," he insisted. "I had some thinking to do. It's not often I get to do that, just think."

She looked up into his handsome face just inches above her. Instantly, it seemed natural to raise her head and brush her lips against his.

Caught off guard, Ben savored the soft sweetness of her. He'd restrained himself from doing this all day. Now, he acknowledged to himself that he couldn't resist her.

A rustling from the kitchen startled Sharon. "Sara's finishing up dinner."

"I'd better go help her," Sharon whispered, stunned by her own boldness but not regretting it.

"We'll talk later," Ben said.

Sharon unsuccessfully searched his eyes for a hint of what he planned to say to her.

She scrambled to her feet. "Yes, I think we have to," she agreed before running off into the kitchen.

"What is it you want to show me?" Sharon asked Ben, her hands buried in the pockets of her coat as she walked beside him down the winding road.

The snow had stopped falling again, but the world was still coated with white. Sharon liked the way it crunched beneath her feet.

Ben shrugged. "You'll see," he said mysteriously. "Besides, I thought you might like one last walk in this precious white stuff."

One last walk in the snow, one last outing with Ben, she thought, her heart aching despite the warm full feeling she had from the feast she'd just consumed at Sara's.

"It makes everything seem so unreal," she observed.

Ben turned and looked at her with probing eyes. "Yes, doesn't it, though?"

Sharon returned his deep glance. He'd said they were to talk, and she assumed this would be their last chance before she was on her way to the airport. She wondered what he planned to say to her that he hadn't already.

An ember of hope flared in her heart, but she didn't dare make too much of it.

She turned her eyes skyward. Although the sun had been struggling to burst through the clouds throughout the day, it had ultimately given in to a gray overcast that made the afternoon seem later than it was.

"Do you think it will snow anymore?" she asked Ben.

He shrugged, glancing up at the sky. "It could I suppose. I guess we should turn on a weather report when we get back and see if it's snowed in Atlanta."

"That's a good idea," she agreed, kicking up a spray of snow with one foot. She looked sideways at him. "I must say this has been a Thanksgiving I won't forget."

"But your plans were ruined."

"I enjoyed being with you and Sara. I only wish she would have let me help her more."

"That's my aunt, independent to the core. You see why she'd so impossible. On one hand, she won't let me do anything for her, yet she complains I don't do enough for her."

Sharon smiled. "Just because she's independent doesn't mean she wants to be alone all the time. I think what she really wants, Ben, is to be allowed to live her own life and still know you care about her. If you go over and eat dinner with her, even though she cooks it, you're doing something for her. She seems awfully fond of you, and proud."

He beamed down on her. "How perceptive you are, Sharon. You just might be right. But I'm afraid once this holiday ends, I'll be lucky to squeeze in enough time for eight hours sleep until after Christmas."

"The fruitcakes," Sharon said with a slow nod. "Maybe you should hire some extra help."

For the first time since she'd met him, some of the easy confidence drained out of his expression.

"I'm afraid I've got all the extra help I can afford. Last year was bad with the recession. And no one knows yet, how this year will be. Two slow Christmases in a row, and we might have to close."

She stopped walking and turned sharply.

"Close your bakery?" she asked incredulously. "What would you do?"

His laugh was hollow. "I haven't thought that far. My concern is for my employees and the survival of this town."

Sharon thought of Glynis and her two sons and the employee whose wife had just had a baby. She understood now, the tremendous burden Ben carried. He was in danger of losing everything important to him, his business, and the well-being of this community.

How little of himself he had left to give, she thought, feeling selfish because she'd hoped for so much from him.

She looked down at the snow. "Do they know what could happen?" she asked.

Ben shook his head. "It's just between you, me and my accountant. I don't want to incite panic about something that might never happen."

Sharon studied the hard set of his jaw and glimpsed the steely determination in his eyes. In her heart she knew if there was a way to get through this, Ben would find it.

His business would require his full attention in the coming months. She wasn't going to complicate matters by asking anything of him.

She pulled her eyes away from him. "I hope you can pull it through," she offered.

"I will," he said. "Come on, we're going to freeze standing here."

"I wish you'd tell me where we're going."

"We're almost there."

He led her down a twisting path. A few hundred yards down, they came to a clearing. Sharon recognized it as a place that had once been a park.

"We took the shortcut," Ben informed her, pointing to the road across the open area. "What do you think?"

Sharon surveyed the sqare plot of land. Except for a swing set with one rusty swing remaining and a cracked chunk of concrete that must have once been a fountain or a pool, it looked like a field.

"I'm sorry, but it looks like your town needs some better parks maintenance."

"Actually the town got in some financial trouble years ago when it built a new ball field and ran out of money. The city council voted to close this park."

Her brow furrowed. "I don't understand..." Then as she glimpsed his expression, she did. He was seeing children playing and families picnicking and flowers growing here.

"You want to reopen it," she guessed.

He smiled. "We have a baseball field and one small park with no playground on the other side of town. Trouble is, we still don't have the money. I think the council will vote me down. They have every year for the past five years."

"Well, it seems if the residents wanted it, they'd convey that to the city council."

"They want it, but they don't want to pay any more taxes. I need some inspiration."

She eyed him incredulously. "You're asking me? I don't know anything about your town."

"But you are intelligent, and don't you sometimes solicit private funds for the museum?"

Sharon bit her lower lip. "I don't know if it will work in this case, but if I were trying to do this, I'd start by making a list of people you know who care enough about this to do something. Get them together, get them excited, and draw up a plan to raise funds, solicit contributions from local businesses and use volunteer labor."

She looked up at him, concluding. "That's how I'd go about it. I'd have to think about it more to draw up a concrete plan."

He nodded, his eyes intent on her.

If he had stood any closer, he would have been touching her, she reflected, as the familiar flame kindled in her heart. Ben worried so much about other people, why didn't he worry more about himself? she wondered.

And with the suddenness of a star falling across the heavens, she knew with deep certainty that impossible as it seemed, she had fallen in love with Ben in these few short days.

Was the park all he had wanted to talk to her about?

She traced the blunt lines of his face with her eyes. She'd never before experienced this deep yearning to be near someone. It confused her, and she didn't know what to do about it.

She couldn't tell him the truth. She couldn't just say, "I love you," then leave. Yet she had to go.

Slowly, he raised his hand and cupped her chin. He felt as though he were holding fine china.

Electricity radiated through her at his touch.

He lowered his mouth nearer to hers. "I wish I could be a knight in shining armor," he said. "But I make a lousy one."

"I don't need rescuing," she insisted. She meant he didn't have to mold himself into an image he didn't think he fit for her.

Ben searched her eyes. In his mind, she was telling him she didn't need him.

But her eyes were still telling him something else. If he kissed her, would she say the same thing?

He prepared to find out, but the sound of a car door slamming from the roadside drew his attention.

With a small frozen gasp, Sharon took a step backward at the sight of the little blue BMW.

Ben's hand dropped to his side, and he eyed her quizzically, his glance shifting between her and the tall, lean man who had emerged from the car and was sliding down the hill toward them.

"It's Chris," she announced under her breath as the intruder reached the bottom of the slope. Then more to herself, she muttered. "What is he doing here?"

She cast a last fleeting look at Ben. If he had anything to say to her, this would be his last chance.

Ben took in the sight of the man crossing the snow-covered field. A shank of hair bounced across his forehead as he walked. He skidded with each step, and Ben guessed the bottoms of his soles were slick, designed more for a carpeted office building than a park in winter. His canvas coat looked too thin to keep out the cold.

A fierce protectiveness rose within Ben. His impulse was to wrap Sharon in his arms and send this stranger away. But he reminded himself he had no right to do that. This other man had every right to take her with him.

He watched incredulously, as Sharon stooped down, picked up a handful of snow, and pelted Chris with it as he approached. It struck him on the right shoulder, ineffective as it disintegrated across the front of his coat.

He looked at Sharon as though she'd mortally wounded him.

"Isn't it wonderful?" she asked.

His dark eyes widened even farther. "Wonderful?"

"The snow!" Sharon replied. "I've never seen any before."

"It makes some darn hazardous driving," he complained. He cast an annoyed look at Ben, then shifted his glance back to Sharon.

"Are you all right?" he asked.

"Of course," she answered. "Didn't you get the message I left your secretary?"

"I called you last night at the number you left, and someone picked up the phone and didn't say anything."

Sharon's head tilted. "You must have had the wrong number. Why didn't you call back?"

"I did, and I got a busy signal."

Sharon remembered the phone ringing last night and Sara saying later the phone had been off the hook. She couldn't imagine anyone doing this intentionally. Then she realized no one could have.

She, Sara, and Ben were the only three in the house when the phone rang.

"There was probably something wrong with the line because of the snow," she suggested.

But Ben knew he had his dog to thank for giving him this day with Sharon. Star hated the sound of the telephone, and if she could reach it, she would knock the receiver off the hook.

He made a mental note to give Star some extra biscuits later.

Chris put his hands to his hips. "I've been worried sick about you. When I told my parents why we weren't coming, they insisted I come and get you myself."

How touching, Sharon thought hollowly. He came after her only because his parents thought he should.

"I'm terribly sorry I disrupted their plans," she apologized.

"Well, as long as you're all right." His glance shifted suspiciously to Ben. "Mrs. Eagleston said I might find you out here."

Sharon wondered whether Sara had wanted to help him find her or had wanted him to find her with Ben. It didn't matter, she supposed.

"I'd like you to meet Ben Russell. I would have truly been stranded if it weren't for his kindness."

Chris's narrowing glance did not reflect gratitude. "Nice to meet you, Ben," he said, offering an ungloved hand.

Ben shook his hand, finding Chris's grip light, quick and insincere. Ben told himself to stop being so judgmental. Under the circumstances, Chris could have been Saint Nicholas himself and he would have found a reason to dislike him.

Still, this man did not seem right for Sharon. Surely she must be able to see that. She'd said she wouldn't marry him, but would she change her mind again once she was home and had forgotten him?

"Thank you for looking out for Sharon," Chris said. Then he reached out and protectively wrapped one arm around her. "I'll take care of her now."

As Sharon's eyes shifted helplessly between the two men, Ben felt his spirits drop with the force of a battleship sinking into the sea.

That's how it was. Chris was here. She was leaving with him, probably relieved to go back to her well-planned life.

He told himself it was best this way; get it over with now. He'd known their parting was inevitable. Still, he hadn't expected it to come so soon.

Chris began walking toward his car, but Sharon held him back.

"My things are at Sara's. And we need to give Ben a ride back there."

But before Chris could reply, Ben said. "I'd rather walk back, if you don't mind."

Sharon's eyes widened. She realized with horror she was not going to see him again.

His gaze locked on hers for a long, silent moment.

Sharon's heart hammered so wildly she feared it would explode.

Chris didn't miss the look that passed between them. He wondered what had happened here.

"It's a long drive back," he prodded her.

Sharon took a last hard loving look at Ben. His image was one of strength and kindness, and she thought that if she had needed the proverbial knight in shining armor, she would have it be no one other than him.

Words failed her. She couldn't bring herself to say good-bye.

As Chris led her across the snow-covered field, Ben waved at her.

Fighting back tears, she waved at him. It was a hollow final gesture to the man who had changed her life forever.

Chapter Nine

In the weeks that followed, Sharon thought frequently of Ben and the quiet friendly town that had embraced her.

Chris accompanied her when she returned the following weekend to get her car. As he maneuvered through the twisting streets, she was surprised at the sense she felt of coming home. Through the car windows, she scanned the streets, secretly hoping to get a glimpse of Ben.

And when the scent of cake baking filled the air, a soft smile rose to her lips.

"I'll bet you're glad to be seeing the last of this place," Chris said after she'd squared things with Mr. Towers and they prepared to get into their individual vehicles.

A knot of regret tightened inside her, and she managed to merely shrug.

147

It seemed to her nothing had changed, and yet everything had.

She'd wasted no time on that snowy Thanksgiving afternoon as they headed toward Pensacola, telling Chris she couldn't marry him. And he had, perhaps deliberately, misunderstood, brushing it off with, "Maybe you're right, it is too soon."

She'd thought over time, he'd realize the truth of what she was saying. But he kept coming around to see her as though nothing had happened, and Sharon began to wonder whether he did really love her.

And she hadn't heard from Ben; she didn't expect to.

She grew more confused than ever.

The Christmas season was in full swing, and the festive garlands and the tree with red bows and sparkling gold ornaments that went up in the museum's lobby only made her heart heavier.

Unexpectedly, Millicent called her in to her office. Sharon's nerves grated as she stepped inside. She wondered if she'd been shirking on her work since she'd returned, even though it was the only thing that seemed to soothe her.

Millicent, confident and blonde, wearing huge black earrings that few would dare to put on, smiled at her over the desktop.

"How are things going?" her boss asked.

Braced for criticism, Sharon told her she thought they were going well and reviewed progress on her recent project. Her smile unfaltering, Millicent nodded as she listened.

"You never miss a detail," she marveled. "And the article on Sara Eagleston shows a side of her no one has ever seen before. I wanted to tell you, I'm definitely impressed.... And a little concerned."

Sharon's head snapped up sharply. "Why?" she asked.

"It's no secret I'm leaving after the first of the year. I've got a stack of resumes in here, but yours isn't among them."

"I'd considered applying," Sharon admitted.

Millicent's smile broadened. "I can't think of anyone I'd like to see take over this job more than you. While I can't make any guarantees, I'd gladly recommend you to the board and be able to walk away knowing the place is in good hands."

"I've decided not to."

Millicent's brow furrowed with concern, and she leaned forward.

"Any particular reason?"

"I don't want to give up what I'm doing now."

Millicent looked thoughtful. "I can understand that. There are days when I'd give anything to get out from behind these doors and actually into the museum. But it's so obvious you believe in this place, Sharon. That's the kind of attitude that's needed for this position. You might be surprised at what you can accomplish if you give it a shot."

"I've thought about it a lot."

Millicent nodded, straightening the stack of applications before her.

"Please think it over one more time. I've got to give these to the board by the beginning of next week. And I would feel better if I could include yours."

"Thanks Millicent, but I doubt I'll change my mind." Sharon rose to leave, but Millicent stopped her with a wave of one hand. "Sharon?" she asked.

"Yes?"

"You've been awfully quiet ever since you were in that accident. Is everything all right?"

"Sure," she replied, convincing herself she wasn't lying because physically she was fine. "I've just had a lot of things on my mind."

Millicent nodded. "Going home for Christmas?"

"I haven't made any plans." She'd visited New Mexico once, but it didn't feel like home and never would. "How about you?"

"Well, I'll be busy moving, so it'll be a pretty rugged holiday."

Sharon nodded understandingly. Millicent had accepted a job with a larger museum in New York. She was one of those people who had an aura of having been born knowing exactly what they want out of life. And sacrificing Christmas to accomodate her goals was merely an inconvenience.

Sharon didn't dare tell Millicent the truth. While she did like her job, she wanted more but didn't know what that consisted of—not Millicent's job though.

That night she went home and rummaged through the closets, searching for the fat black folder that had been delivered to her from a lawyer's office. She sat at the white-topped counter in her apartment and pulled the papers out, one-by-one.

Amid the mass of legal papers, she pulled out a sheet of paper printed in neat, tiny letters. Across the top in capital letters it said, "THE BEST FRUITCAKE IN GEORGIA."

Propping her head on one arm, Sharon bit her lip and laughed softly, tears filling her eyes as she realized her grandfather had written this. She tried to envision him sitting at a desk and carefully penning the list of ingredients.

Maybe he'd chuckled himself over his grandiose claim.

She rubbed a palm against the folds of her sweatsuit. There were many more papers to dig through.

She hesitated. A fear cropped up inside her that maybe she was going to find something she'd rather not know about, something about her grandfather's dealings with Ben's grandfather.

A gnawing in her stomach reminded her she'd eaten only a cup of yogurt for lunch.

Abandoning the papers, she went to the refrigerator, pulled out a frozen dinner, and popped it in the microwave.

Raking one hand through her hair, she turned to face the papers on the counter. Everything that had gone wrong in her life she attributed to her own fears. All she had was this precious little connection to her grandfather, and she wasn't going to ignore it any longer, despite her feelings for Ben. She had to know the truth.

Resolutely, she returned to her stool and continued sorting through the papers, amazed to find more recipes. He must have written down all those he'd used in his restaurant.

Distractedly, she left them only long enough to fetch her dinner from the oven when the timer rang. She was thoughtfully scanning a recipe for lemon meringue pie and munching a forkful of meatloaf when the sound of the doorbell startled her.

She found Chris at the front door, holding a Santa Claus figure.

The sight was so unexpected, she laughed out loud.

"Are you going to let me in or what?" he asked, closing his arm around the figure as though he were trying to hide it.

She stepped aside and gestured for him to enter.

"What is that?" she asked.

"A guy came around the office selling them today for the 'Help Our Children' charity. I thought you could use some Christmas cheer around here."

He scanned her living room. Sharon followed his eyes through the small area tastefully decorated with a floral print sofa, lilac carpet, and glass-topped tables. A framed watercolor accented one wall.

Sharon had taken great care in decorating her apartment. It wasn't like her, she realized, not to have brought out by now her prized collection of Christmas decorations.

"I guess I have neglected the season," she conceded, motioning for him to place Santa on an end table. "It was sweet of you to think of me, and to help out the needy kids."

And something she never would have expected of him, she reflected. Had he perhaps understood her more than he let on? Did he care enough to try to change her mind?

They needed to discuss this, she realized. It wasn't fair of her to allow him to continue misunderstanding her feelings.

Chris plugged in the decoration and smiled at the soft, festive glow. "Now it's at least beginning to look a little like Christmas in here."

Sharon cast him a grateful smile. "Thank you," she said sincerely. "Can I get you something to drink?"

"A cola if you have one. Actually, I just stopped by to see if you'd eaten yet." His expression darkened. "We haven't seen much of each other lately."

Sharon pointed apologetically to her half-eaten dinner in the cardboard tray on the counter. "I can heat one up for you. Actually, as long as you're here, I'd like you to have a look at something."

"What's that?"

His eyes were already fastened on the pile of papers on the counter.

"My grandfather's papers. When I got them,

I was still too hurt, thinking he didn't care about me, to look them over."

Chris shed his coat, clearly in his element now as he sat on a bar stool and began rifling through the stack of papers.

"What are these? Recipes?" he asked.

"He owned a restaurant. Turkey, salisbury steak or meatloaf?" she asked as she rummaged through the contents of her freezer."

"Turkey," he answered without enthusiasm.

While she prepared the frozen tray for the oven, she related the story of the fruitcake factory and how her grandfather had been a co-owner before his death.

Finally, she turned to Chris and rubbed her chin. "There's something that bothers me about all this."

"What's that?" Chris asked.

"If these recipes legally belong to Ben's family, why would my grandfather have taken such pains to save them for me? I mean, Ben says my grandfather gave away everything in his restaurant. Apparently, he didn't believe anything he had was worth much, except these. And why did he give them to me and not my sister?"

"Maybe we'll find some clue in these other papers."

Sharon put his dinner in the oven, set the

timer and sat down beside him. "I can't understand them."

Chris grinned. "But I can," he offered. "If you want me to."

Sharon mulled over the prospects. Whatever the truth was, she knew it wouldn't affect her feelings for Ben. And if her grandfather had been cheated, it didn't mean she had to demand justice and disrupt Ben's life with his business being on shaky ground already.

Or had her grandfather given her these because he knew he would be cheated and wanted to give her the power to stop it? Could she just drop it and diminish what it had taken him a lifetime to build?

But if there was compensation involved, her sister and her sister's children were concerned here. If she discovered the truth, she'd inevitably be bound to contact Blake. She owed her older sister too much to keep this from her.

Her head began to throb. She leaned over the counter, cradling her forehead in the palm of her hand.

The pressure of Chris's hand on her shoulder was unexpected.

She looked up at him.

"If an injustice was done, you can't just ignore it," he advised her softly.

Sharon stared at Chris and felt a stabbing in

her heart. Despite the realities he saw everyday, the things he had to deal with that seemingly had nothing to do with justice or freedom, he remained an idealist. She supposed that was what had drawn her to him in the first place. At that moment, she wished she did love him, but she knew she never could.

It was Ben her weary heart craved. "I don't know if you want to help me with this, Chris," she blurted. "Maybe you shouldn't be here at all."

She recognized his well-practiced look of cool determination. She hoped she would never have to face him in a courtroom as a hostile witness.

"You haven't been the same since you got back from Georgia," he observed dryly.

"I told you things had changed, Chris. I tried to tell you."

He withdrew his hand, pulling it slowly back.

"You said we shouldn't get married right away. I agree."

Sharon glanced up at the ceiling in frustration. She didn't want to hurt Chris. He'd never been less than good to her. But she had to make herself clear.

Her eyes dropped back on him.

"I think I fell in love with Ben," she confessed.

Chris nodded slowly as though he'd heard a grim verdict. "The guy in the park."

She shook her head. "He wasn't just someone in the park. He was kind and helpful."

Chris leaned forward, at last shedding some of his lawyer's composure.

"You hardly know him. I realize this is partly my fault. I get so wrapped up in my work. Sometimes I don't do a good job of showing you how I feel. I think you're making a mistake if you're willing to throw away all our years together because you took a second look at someone else."

Sharon bit her lip. Why did he have to be so rational?

"I don't mind your commitment to your work. I admire it."

"Are you going to see Ben again?"

She shook her head. "No."

"Then I don't understand."

Searching Chris's eyes, Sharon recalled the thrill she felt when Ben was near. How even now she wished it were Ben here with her. "I liked him a lot. It made me question my commitment to you."

"I think the fact that you're saying you're not going to see him again answers that."

"That's not because of you."

Chris blanched as though she'd struck him.

She expected him to get up and walk out.

"I know I've put a lot of pressure on you lately about Millicent's job and going to meet my family. Are you telling me to get out of your life, Sharon?"

"I'm trying to be honest with you, Chris. I just don't know if there's a future for us."

He nodded solemnly. "Message delivered. Do we just go on from here?"

Her heart as bewildered as her mind, Sharon wondered now if maybe she did love Chris in a different way. Maybe it wasn't as fast and furious as what she'd felt for Ben, but maybe Chris was right. Maybe Ben's attraction was that he was someone new and unattainable.

"I don't know," she answered honestly.

Chris gave her a long, hard appraisal. "I'm not going to press you into saying something you might regret later. What about the papers, do you want me to take them to the office with me?"

"Yes," she answered slowly.

Chris grinned. "So this guy hasn't got you so dazzled you're going to back off?"

"I just want to know the truth. I'm not saying I want to act on it."

"Fair enough."

The oven timer rang, startling them both. Sharon looked at Chris, then they both laughed. The tension between them shattered like glass.

"I think I've lost my appetite," he admitted, sifting through the papers.

"Can I keep the recipes here?"

He began pulling them out of the pile.

Within minutes, he was preparing to leave. Sharon slid off her stool to walk him to the door and glanced at the glowing Santa lamp.

"Thanks for the Santa," she said.

"Maybe next time we can go crazy and put up a tree," he suggested.

"I'd like that," Sharon replied as she unlocked the door.

"Good." He brushed his lips to hers.

As she watched him walk down the corridor, Sharon raised fingertips to her mouth. Her heart grew heavy as she quietly compared the excitement of Ben's kiss to the cool lingering feeling Chris's had left and realized how deeply she yearned to sample Ben's once again.

I've got to be crazy, Sharon thought as she surveyed the neat row of ingredients on the counter before her. As much as she'd helped her aunt in the kitchen as a teenager, she'd never baked a cake before in her life, except occasionally one from a mix.

And here she was about to undertake what was supposedly the best fruitcake in all Georgia. She was determined to have it come out as her grandfather had intended it when he devised the recipe.

She thought of the call she'd made to Georgia

earlier in the day and Glynis's agreement to fulfill her strange request. When Sharon had asked her not to tell Ben about it, Glynis hadn't actually committed herself. Sharon had quickly apologized that she couldn't say more, and hoped Glynis would remain silent.

Futilely, she slid a large mixing bowl before her. Such an enormous and painstaking task. But she knew it was one she must complete.

Thoughtfully, she got up, walked to the stereo, and spent several minutes thumbing through her stack of cassettes. She hadn't the money to convert her music to compact discs as Chris had. Finally, she found what she was searching for and loaded a tape in the player.

The tiny peal of chimes preceded the familiar Christmas carol. Sharon smiled. On her way back to the kitchen, she stopped and plugged in the Santa lamp. One way or another, she was going to work up some Christmas spirit.

As the sound of carols rang through the apartment, she set to the task before her.

Meticulous in her measurements and mixing, Sharon gained a new appreciation for Ben's ability to turn out thousands of these fruitcakes in one day.

Amazingly, within an hour, she had the cake in the oven and was gathering bowls and utensils for the dishwasher. The aroma wafting from the oven brought thoughts of Ben as strongly as his aftershave would have.

She sat on the couch, closed her eyes, and envisioned his face. Did he, she wondered, think of her at all?

The ringing of the phone broke through her reverie.

"Hello?" she answered.

"Sharon?" It was Chris. "I think we've got something."

"I am so happy you could come for the weekend," Blake told Sharon as she rounded the kitchen table with a plate of cookies. She set them before Sharon, then dropped into a chair.

"The ones with the puddles of chocolate in the middle are the best," Blake advised.

Sharon studied her sister. She was tall and trim, with long dark hair she wore tied back loosely with a scarf. Her eyes always sparkled, and even in her jeans and white shirt, she looked more like a fashion model than the mother of two preschoolers.

Sharon obligingly sampled one. Blake's house smelled of cocoa and chocolate and cinnamon. Down to the red and green dishtowels, every corner of the house was decorated for the holiday. From here she could see the glow of the lights from the tree in the living room and more colored lights along the outside windows.

"I wish we'd grown up in a house like this," Sharon told her sister. She sipped on the generous glass of eggnog her sister had given her.

"I take that as the highest compliment," her sister replied with her usual bright, easy smile. "And I do wish you lived closer so you could come more often."

"You and Ralph would get tired of having me around."

"I doubt that."

Sharon looked down at the wooden tabletop. "Besides, I have my own life to live. I can't just move into yours."

Blake nodded. "It'll happen. Give it time. Ralph and I have been lucky."

"I met someone, Blake. But it's a long, complicated story. And in a way it involves you and Ralph."

Blake's bright eyes narrowed as she puzzled over her sister's last sentence.

"Well, the kids are in bed and Ralph's watching 'A Christmas Carol,' so shoot, Kid."

Sharon laughed. It was hard to know where to begin, but then she supposed it started with the moment her path had crossed Ben's.

Half an hour later, Blake was staring across the table at her open-mouthed.

"Chris says since we have the recipes in our possession, the burden will be on Ben to prove they're legally his."

"You're in love with him, but you're going to sue him?"

She shook her head. "I don't want to sue him, I want to help him. I've already made about twenty fruitcakes and given out his brochures with the samples. He's getting lots of orders."

"Why don't you just offer to help him?"

"I don't think he'd accept my help. But the point is, if there's a lawsuit to be filed, it's not just my decision. It's yours too."

Blake's gaze grew distant. "I don't want his money. But if his grandfather stole those recipes from our grandfather, I think the world should know."

"That's what Chris says too."

Blake turned her eyes on her younger sister. "Our grandfather's dead, and nothing is going to change the fact he didn't have anything to do with us when we needed him. The fact that he left all this for us to figure out only reflects his selfishness. I think, Sharon, that if you were to drop this, it wouldn't really matter. Not if it's going to stand between you and the man you've fallen in love with."

Sharon drummed her fingers against the still-full glass of eggnog. "You've got your family right here, Blake. Maybe I need to understand this more than you do. And nothing's going to come of what I felt for Ben. I don't think he's gotten over the death of his first wife."

Blake gave her a long, low look. "Do what you think is best, Sharon. Just remember you've a long time to live with the results."

Chapter Ten

Sharon rushed through the stone corridors of the museum, her heels clicking against the buffed linoleum, the blazer of her tweed suit hanging to one side and a silk scarf dangling precariously from her swept back hair.

She hated Monday morning traffic. She hated being late. It got her whole week off to a bad start. Nothing seemed to be going right for her lately.

"Ms. Hunicutt," Millicent's secretary, Joan, called out as Sharon zipped past her desk toward her office. Technically, Joan was her secretary too, but Sharon always thought of her as belonging to Millicent's realm.

Sharon backed up. "Good morning, Joan," she greeted her belatedly, repentant for having stormed by without speaking. There was no point in taking her ill mood out on other people.

Joan smiled accommodatingly. She knew
Sharon must have something on her mind and
wasn't offended by having been slighted.

"There's someone in your office waiting to see
you." The secretary kept her voice low.

Sharon looked puzzled, shooting a glance toward the closed door of her office. "Who is it?"
She couldn't imagine Joan allowing a visitor
into her office in her absence.

"Sara Eagleston. I asked her to wait in the
lobby, but she insisted on going inside."

Sharon glanced again at her office door. What
was Sara doing here? She knew the woman sel-
dom traveled beyond the confines of her hometown. She'd indicated that when Sharon had all
but begged her to come for the opening of her
exhibit.

She looked back at Joan. "It's all right," she
assured her, then proceeded toward her office.
She stopped just before reaching the door, realizing what a wreck she was. Taking a quick
inventory, she straightened her blazer and se-
cured the scarf in her hair before entering.

Sara was seated in the single leather chair, a
styrofoam cup of coffee in her hand.

Had something happened to Ben? Sharon worried, concern mingling with the pleasure of
seeing her friend again.

She leaned over and hugged the small woman, mindful of the coffee cup.

"It's good to see you again, Sara. What on earth are you doing here?" she asked finally.

Sara set her coffee cup on the desktop. "You have a lovely museum here, but this isn't the best coffee."

Sharon wrinkled her nose. "I could have warned you about that. But you didn't come for coffee. You haven't changed your mind about the exhibit, have you?"

"Mercy, no. First off, I came to see how you were faring, since my nephew's too stubborn to come."

Sharon averted her eyes. "He's busy right now."

Sara nodded slowly. "He's always busy. That's how he shuts the world out, you know."

"How is he?" Sharon asked, her voice thready.

"He's miserable, but he won't admit it. In the few days you were at my house, Sharon, you put a fire back into him I hadn't seen in years. He needs you."

Sharon moved toward her desk and shuffled a handful of brochures. "If that were the case, he would tell me."

Sara appraised her thoughtfully. Finally, she opened her pocketbook and extracted a long white envelope.

She held it out to Sharon.

"Glynis tells me the bakery's been getting a lot of orders from this part of the country."

Sharon raised one eyebrow and folded her arms. "So?"

"So why are you selling Ben's fruitcakes for him?"

"I wanted to repay him. He was kind to me. Besides, the fruitcakes are good. People like them."

"You brought some back with you?"

"I made some. I found my grandfather's recipes."

Still holding out the envelope, Sara nodded. "Yes, your grandfather had a flair with food. I shouldn't have left without telling you about him. Take this."

Sharon accepted the envelope, staring at it but not opening it.

Suddenly, she looked up at Sara. "You know more about my grandfather than you've said," she accused.

"I know he was no old fool. He was a shrewd, ingenious man who got lax in his grief. He wouldn't accept a flat payment for his recipes. He insisted on a share of the profits. But at the time that was no substantial amount. When he died, no one tried too hard to find anyone to make payments to."

Sharon's arms dropped to her sides. "You knew this and you didn't tell me?"

"It was a mistake," Sara confessed. "Ben doesn't think I know what shaky ground his company is on. I planned to tell him the truth, but when I saw you two together, how happy he was, I was afraid he'd let a decades-old business scandal destroy what he'd found with you."

"So you never told him?"

"He doesn't know. The proof you need is in that envelope. Don't ask me how I got it. You can use it as you see fit. There's a letter in there detailing how all this came about. Please don't read it until after I've left. I'm too ashamed."

Sharon eyed the older women quizzically. She couldn't imagine the kind, graceful woman ever having done anything she'd be embarrassed to admit.

Sara rose, leaving Sharon staring at the sealed envelope.

"You know," she said. "Ben will go on brooding his life away before he'd ask anyone to make what he considers a sacrifice. He needs someone who is willing to shake him up." She shook her head. "It's not my place to say, but I'm old enough to know when I see two people who can't get enough of one another, even if they're both too stubborn to admit it. There are some things in life you've got to just grab onto. It's like catching a butterfly."

She was gone before Sharon could stop her.

Sharon looked down at the envelope, unsure she wanted to explore the contents. Rounding her desk, she realized she'd been pacing throughout the length of Sara's visit. She sank into her chair and stared at the empty seat where Sara had been. Suddenly, she knew what she had to do. Darn Sara, why did she have to be so right?

The sky was dark on the late winter afternoon when Sharon pulled her car into the gravel parking lot of the bakery. The snow was gone now, and she spied Ben's black truck near the door.

She should have been tired after the long drive from Pensacola. Instead, she felt refreshed, elated, but apprehensive just the same. Her heart lurched at the enormity of what she was doing. But the thought of seeing Ben again spurred her on. She never wanted to leave him. That one thing at least was clear in her mind. But she didn't know how he would react to that.

Knowing she had to at least try, she maneuvered her car into a vacant space.

She got out and walked toward the building.

As she opened the front door, the sound of piped-in carols and aroma of spices assaulted her. For the first time, she began to feel some of the joyous anticipation of the holiday season.

Glynis looked up from her desk, her face growing animated as she recognized Sharon. She jumped up, rounded the desk, and greeted her with a friendly hug.

"Am I ever glad you're here. Ben's been a bear since you left."

Sharon laughed lightly. She couldn't imagine Ben being a bear, ever.

"How are you, Glynis?" Sharon asked.

"Fine. Gee, you look great."

"Is Ben here?"

Glynis's merry expression darkened, and Sharon followed her glance to the door of Ben's office to see him filling the door frame. His eyes raked over her.

A sweet warmth coursed through her body at the sight of him. He looked taller, stronger, more handsome than she remembered.

"Hello, Sharon," he addressed her, not moving. His expression revealed nothing. Was he angry at her for coming here?

"Ben." His name escaped her dry lips.

"What brings you here?" he asked.

"Business," she answered. Did he seem relieved, or was she only imagining it?

He simply nodded.

When she said nothing, he asked, "Don't tell me we have another artist living here?"

"It has nothing to do with the museum. Is there somewhere we can talk?"

Glynis glanced nervously around the room. "I need to go make some photocopies..." She reached for a stack of papers on the desktop.

Ben held one palm in the air to stop her frantic motions. "Never mind, Glynis. I was just on my way out, and I'm already late." He returned his glance to Sharon. "You'll have to come with me if you want to talk."

"All right," Sharon agreed. "Where are we going?"

"To the town's annual Christmas parade. Just leave your car here," he instructed.

As Sharon walked with him out to his truck, she wondered if she'd made a huge mistake in coming here. She loved a parade as much as anyone, but was watching one so important he couldn't spare her a few minutes first?

She watched his profile in the dim light as he drove. If he was happy to see her, he hadn't shown any sign of it.

She took an envelope out of her portfolio and sat it on the seat beside him.

"What's that?" he asked.

"The plan," she volunteered.

"Plan?"

"For the park. Remember, I told you I could work one out if I had the time to think about it."

Ben gave her a sidelong glance, then turned his eyes back to the road. "You drove all the way from Florida to give me this?"

"You're still interested in rejuvenating the park, aren't you?"

"You shouldn't have come."

Sharon blanched. He might as well have shot her with a cannon.

"Why not?"

Ben hadn't been able to stop thinking about her all the time she was gone. Seeing her again, he didn't see how he was going to keep from pouring out his feelings, asking her to stay. And what could he offer her? Good intentions? Those were never enough.

"I shouldn't have to explain it."

He pulled into a parking lot.

Sharon saw a lot of people standing around the streets, but no parade. She remembered the first night she'd been here, standing in the street with Ben by her side. She'd felt so alone and lost then. Now she knew right here with him was where she wanted to be.

"Where's the parade? I thought we came to watch one."

Ben laughed explosively. He wrapped an arm around her shoulders and drew her closer.

"Not exactly, darling," he said, leading her toward a Model A Ford parked at the curb. "We're in it."

Her pulse sped at the easy way he'd called her darling. Had he realized what he'd said?

The driver of the car, a round, bald man in overalls and an unzipped black parka, got out and walked to meet them. "I was starting to get worried about you, Mr. Russell. You were supposed to be here fifteen minutes ago."

"Sorry, Hank, I got held up. Hank Colridge, this is Sharon Hunicutt. Ms. Hunicutt will be riding with us."

Hank nodded his head in her direction. "Pleasure to meet you, Ma'am. Hop aboard. The parade's about to start. Can't have folks wondering where the mayor is."

Sharon headed for the car door. She'd never ridden in a parade before, nor in an antique car, but she didn't care where she was as long as she got to talk to Ben. What she had to say was important.

Before she touched the door handle, Ben caught hold of her and guided her toward the rear rumble seat.

"We ride up here," he said.

Sharon hesitated, then shrugged. If nothing

else, she was a good sport. As he hoisted her into the seat, she was aware of his strong hands gripping her waist.

This was crazy. As she sat in the open rear seat, watching costumed clowns drift down the street and listening to the distant strains of a band playing "Santa Claus Is Coming to Town," she wondered if Chris and Millicent had been right when they told her she was insane to come up here like this.

She thought of Chris, the talk they'd had last night. It had hurt her, making him see she could never be what he wanted, letting go because it was selfish and destructive to hold on. At least, she felt, they'd parted as friends.

Her eyes sparkled under the street lamp as she gazed down on Ben.

"Who's going to help you up here?" she teased.

He climbed into the seat with amazing agility for a man his size.

As he eased himself into the small space beside her he finally turned. "I'm sorry, I didn't hear you," he said pointedly.

"Never mind," Sharon replied, mindful of how close together they were squeezed in the confines of the small seat.

She watched as Hank, satisfied they were secure in the rumble seat, got in on the driver's side and started the car. Its engine vibrated softly.

"This has been remarkably restored," she noted.

Ben nodded. "Hank doesn't let just anyone ride in it. This car belonged to his father. It sat in a barn for about twenty years before he decided to start working on it."

He eyed her keenly, and warmth swept through her, despite the cold wind that was blowing.

"You didn't come to talk about cars or to ride in a parade," he said. "Or to give me a plan for restoring the park," he added.

"No," she agreed. "I didn't. I came to talk about us."

A light flashed in his eyes. He spoke slowly. "It's been all I could do to keep from charging down to Florida and begging you to come back," he confessed.

Sharon reeled at the enormity of his admission. "Why didn't you?" she insisted.

He started to speak, but before he could get the words out, a sharp jerk let them know the parade had started. The car was moving.

He cast her a quick sidelong glance. "Just wave and smile," he instructed.

Sharon frowned. She didn't care about the parade or anything else except what Ben had just said to her.

She glanced down at her jeans, sweater and corduroy jacket, panicking as the car turned and she spotted the dense crowd lining the street. She certainly wasn't dressed to be in a parade.

"Just smile," Ben repeated through a frozen grin. "We'll talk later." He followed with another sentence, but she couldn't hear him.

"What?" she demanded over the growing din of the parade, leaning closer.

He leaned toward her, his breath caressing her ear. "I said, I love you."

Sharon stared up at him with round, wondrous eyes.

Ben grinned sheepishly.

A brilliant smile set her face aglow.

She longed to reach out and throw her arms around him and almost did until she remembered the crowd.

The music, whistles, sirens, and faces all became a blur that threatened to never end. Sharon was aware only of Ben close beside her, as she wanted him always to be.

But there was one piece of news she had for him that might have him recanting his words before the night was over.

She bit her lip, praying she wouldn't lose him,

lose the love that was more precious than anything she'd ever known.

At last, the parade ended. Ben helped her climb down from her perch, quickly mumbling a thank you to Hank, and leading her by the hand down the darkened street.

"Where are we going?" she asked as they wove through vehicles scattered in a church parking lot off the main street.

He turned behind an empty horse trailer, pulling her after him.

"This will do for now," he said, folding her immediately into his arms and kissing her powerfully, unleashing the love that had been building between them since the first moment they met.

Sharon sank into his embrace, his muscular body sheltering her from the cold night. At last, she had found something in life that was truly hers, a kind of love some people only wish for. Never again would she feel lost or alone or orphaned. For the first time, she felt truly alive, no longer just going through the motions. She knew what she wanted. She knew it was worth all the pain of waiting her whole life for it.

Ben pressed her head to his chest. "There's not a moment since you left I haven't been thinking about you."

She leaned back, probing deeply into his rich, warm eyes.

"Why didn't you tell me?"

"I thought you didn't want to be here."

She laughed softly, blinking back a sudden onslaught of threatening tears. "It's the first place I've ever felt at home."

"Why didn't you tell me?"

"I didn't think you were over Yvonne."

He smoothed her hair. "What I was not over was imposing a life on her she didn't want and making us both unhappy. I was afraid of making the same mistake again."

"And if I were to come here of my own free will?"

"I'd cherish you forever. Marry me, Sharon. I don't want to be without you again." He knew suddenly it was a promise he was capable of carrying through with great joy.

She stepped back, wriggling free of his embrace to clear her mind.

He looked stunned.

"What's wrong?" he asked.

"There's one more thing I have to tell you, and you might change your mind when I do."

His expression grew solemn. "What is it, Sharon?"

She averted her eyes.

"Your grandfather cheated mine. I have proof."

"That doesn't affect the way I feel about you."

"My grandfather and his heirs are entitled to ten percent of Russell Bakery's profits."

He stared down at her. "I had no idea, Sharon. I swear."

"You couldn't have known. Sara hid the paperwork all these years."

He shot her an incredulous frown. "Sara? Why?" escaped his lips.

"She didn't find it until after your grandfather's death. Your father was less than keen on trying to run the factory and having problems with his marriage. She was afraid it would be the final straw to send him packing. As time went on and no heirs showed up to claim my grandfather's share, the idea of coming clean slipped further and further from her mind."

Perplexed, Ben rubbed his jaw. "But when you told her you were Devan's granddaughter, she denied knowing anything about his part in the business."

"Because she was afraid it would come between us. And now I'm afraid it has."

He studied her evenly, looking angry. "If I owe you and your family money, I'll make good on it somehow. I can't believe Sara deceived us both."

She shook her head. "My sister and I agree we don't want the money. Sara did it because she loves you. I think I understand."

His voice filtered through the night air. "What do you want, Sharon?"

"I want my grandfather to get credit for developing his recipes. And I want to actively take over his ten percent of the company. I want to work on marketing your product. You have too many other things to do."

His eyes leveled on her. "This doesn't make sense. Once we're married, it will be your company too."

"I don't want it because it's yours and your family's. I want it because of my grandfather. You don't understand because you've spent all your life engulfed by family. I've spent my life searching for one."

He startled her by meshing her into his arms again, holding her tightly.

"This is a place where you'll always be loved and wanted. It's a promise I can honestly make now, one I should have made weeks ago. But I'd better warn you what you're getting into."

She looked up at him with moist, silvery eyes.

"I told you this would be a rough year. The season's not over, and despite the sudden surge of sales in northern Florida, we're just going to barely scrape by. You're in for a wild time if you're signing on with me."

She beamed up at him. "I've never looked forward to anything more. Besides, I don't want the company and the city government taking up all your time."

He narrowed his gaze. "And what about your time? Will the company take all of it?"

She hesitated. "I don't want it to. I mean, since we're both so intent on maintaining our family legacies, there should be some point to it."

He graced her with a wide grin. Her heart fluttered as it had the first time she set eyes on that devilish, dashing face.

"Like a big family of our own?" he asked.

"Something like that."

"Something exactly like that," he asserted. He kissed her solidly, and Sharon felt contentment settle over her heart.

The brassy sound of "We Wish You a Merry Christmas" broke through the stillness, and she looked up to see uniformed members of the high school band straggling back toward the adjacent church.

"The happiest of holidays," Ben said quietly. "Let's go before we're discovered."

"Should we go tell Sara?"

"Not now. There will be time enough to make our announcement to the world later."

With her hand planted solidly in his, she walked off with him into the cold Georgia night.

Her spirits were high and her heart beat in time to the festive music that cut through the distance. This was just the beginning of a holiday that would last the rest of their lives.